THE CASES OF
CHASE AND DELACROIX

In the Great Depression, millionaire polymath Abel Chase and his associate, Claire Delacroix, are requested to investigate the San Francisco Police Department's most baffling cases: an actor found dead in his locked dressing room, with two tiny punctures in his neck; a deep-water explorer who disappears from his diving suit, sixty feet beneath the surface of Monterey Bay; and a test pilot who, on a flight with her passenger in an experimental fighter plane, emerges from cloud cover — alone!

Books by Richard A. Lupoff
in the Linford Mystery Library:

THE UNIVERSAL HOLMES

RICHARD A. LUPOFF

THE CASES OF CHASE AND DELACROIX

LINFORD
Leicester

First published in Great Britain

First Linford Edition
published 2012

British Library CIP Data

Lupoff, Richard A., *1935* –
   The cases of Chase and Delacroix. - -
(Linford mystery library)
   1. Detective and mystery stories, American.
   2. Large type books.
   I. Title II. Series
   813.5′4–dc23

   ISBN 978–1–4448–1257–2

Published by
F. A. Thorpe (Publishing)
Anstey, Leicestershire

Set by Words & Graphics Ltd.
Anstey, Leicestershire
Printed and bound in Great Britain by
T. J. International Ltd., Padstow, Cornwall

This book is printed on acid-free paper

1

The Case of the Vampire's Victim

The great Bosendörfer piano responded eagerly to Abel Chase's practiced hands, its crashing notes echoing from the high, raftered ceiling of the music room. Beyond the tall, westward-facing windows, the January night was dark and wind-swept. The lights of the college town of Berkeley, California, sparkled below, and beyond the black face of the bay, the more garish illumination of San Francisco shimmered seductively.

The sweet tones of the Guarnarius violin bowed by Chase's confidante and associate, Claire Delacroix, dashed intricately among the piano chords. Clad in shimmering silver, Claire offered a dramatic contrast to Chase's drab appearance. Her platinum hair, worn in the soft style of an earlier age, cascaded across the gracefully rounded shoulders that emerged from her silvery, bias-cut gown; a single diamond, suspended from a delicate silver chain, glittered in the hollow of her throat. Her deep-set eyes, a blue so dark as at times to appear almost purple, shone with a rare intelligence.

Abel Chase's hair was as dark as Claire's was pale, save for the patches of snow which appeared at the temples. Chase wore a neatly-trimmed black moustache in which only a few light-colored hairs were interspersed. He was clad in a pale, soft-collared shirt and a tie striped with the colors of his alma mater, a silken dressing gown and the trousers of his customary midnight blue suit. His expression was saturnine.

'Enough, Delacroix.' He ceased to play, and she lowered her bow and instrument. 'Stravinsky has outdone himself,' Chase allowed. 'A few corrections and suggestions, notably to the second *eclogue*, and his manuscript will be ready for return. His *cantiléne* and *gigue* are most affecting, while the *dithyrambe* is a delight. After his more ambitious orchestral pieces of recent years, it is fascinating to see him working on so small a canvas.'

Chase had risen from the piano bench and taken two long strides toward the window when the room's freshly restored silence was shattered by the shrilling of a telephone bell. Chase whirled and started toward the machine, but his associate had lifted the delicate French-styled instrument from its cradle. She murmured into it, paused, then added a few words and held the instrument silently toward her companion.

'Yes.'

He held the instrument, his eyes glittering with interest. He raised his free hand and brushed a fingertip along the edge of his moustache. After a time he murmured, 'Definitely dead? Very well. Yes, you were right to reseal the room. I shall come over shortly. Now, quickly, the address.' He continued to hold the telephone handset to his ear, listening and nodding, then grunted and returned it to its cradle.

'Delacroix, I am going to the city. Please fetch your wrap, I shall need you to drive me to the dock. And perhaps you

3

would care to assist me. In that case, I urge you to dress warmly, as a light snowfall has been falling for several hours — a most unusual event for San Francisco.' Without waiting for a response he strode to his own room, hung his dressing gown carefully in a cedar-lined closet and donned his suit coat.

Claire Delacroix awaited him in the flagstone-floored foyer. She had slipped into a sable jacket and carried an elegant purse woven of silvery metal links so fine as to suggest cloth. Chase removed an overcoat from a rack beside the door, slipped into its warm confines, and lifted hat and walking stick from their places.

Shortly a powerful Hispano-Suiza snaked its way through the winding, darkened roads of the Berkeley hills, Claire Delacroix behind the wheel, Abel Chase seated beside her, a lap robe warming him against the wintry chill.

'I suppose you'd like to know what this is about,' Chase offered.

'Only as much as you wish to tell me,' Claire Delacroix replied.

'That was Captain Baxter on the

4

telephone,' Chase told her.

'I knew as much. I recognized his gruff voice, for all that Baxter dislikes to speak to women.'

'You misjudge him, Delacroix. That's merely his manner. He has a wife and five daughters to whom he is devoted.'

'You may be right. Perhaps he has his fill of women at home. I suppose he's got another juicy murder for you, Abel.'

Chase's moustache twitched when Claire Delacroix called him by his familiar name. He was well aware that it would have been futile to ask her to address him by his given name, Akhenaton, and Claire Delacroix knew him far too intimately to refer to him as Doctor Chase. Still, 'Abel' was a name few men were permitted to use in conversation with him, and no woman save for Claire Delacroix.

'The man is distraught. He seems to think that a vampire has struck in San Francisco, draining the blood of a victim and leaving him for dead.'

Claire Delacroix laughed, the silvery sound snatched away on the wind. 'And will the victim then rise and walk, a new recruit to the army of the undead?'

'You scoff,' Chase commented.

'I do.'

There was a momentary pause, then Chase said, 'As do I. Baxter is at the site. He has studied the circumstances of the crime and concluded that it is impossible, by any normal means. Therefore and *ipso facto*, the solution must be supernatural.'

'You of course disagree.'

'Indeed. The very term *supernatural* contradicts itself. The Universe encompasses all objects and events. If a thing has occurred, it is necessarily not supernatural. If it were supernatural, it could not occur.'

'Then we are confronted with an impossible crime,' Claire Delacroix stated.

Abel Chase shook his head in annoyance. 'Again, Delacroix, a contradiction in terms. That which is impossible cannot happen. That which happens is therefore, of necessity, possible. No,' he snorted, 'this crime is neither supernatural nor impossible, no matter that it may seem to be either — or both. I intend to unravel this tangled skein. Remain at my side if you will, and be instructed!'

The dark, winding road had debouched by now into the town's downtown district. On a Saturday night during the academic year warmly clad undergraduates stood in line to purchase tickets for talkies. The young intellectuals in their cosmopolitanism chose among the sensuality of Marlene Dietrich in *The Blue Angel*, the collaborative work of the geniuses Dali and Buñuel in *L'Age d'Or*, the polemics of the Ukrainian Dovzhenko's *Zemlya*, and the simmering rage of Edward G. Robinson in *Little Caesar*. Young celebrants gestured and exclaimed at the unusual sight of snowflakes falling from the January sky. Their sportier (or wealthier) brethren cruised the streets in Bearcats and Auburns. The Depression might have spread fear and want throughout the land, but the college set remained bent on the pursuit of loud jazz and illicit booze.

Claire Delacroix powered the big, closed car down the sloping avenue that led to the city's waterfront, where Abel Chase's power boat rode at dock, lifting and falling with each swell of the bay's cold, brackish water.

Climbing from the car, Chase carefully folded his lap robe and placed it on the seat. He turned up the collar of his warm overcoat, drew a pair of heavy gloves from a pocket and donned them. Together, he and Claire Delacroix crossed to a wooden shed built out over the bay. Chase drew keys from his trouser pocket, opened a heavy lock, and permitted Claire to enter before him. They descended into a powerful motor boat. Chase started the engine and they roared from the shed, heading toward the San Francisco Embarcadero. The ferries had stopped running for the night. Tramp steamers and great commercial freighters stood at anchor in the bay. The powerboat wove among them trailing an icy, greenish-white wake.

Steering the boat with firm assurance, Chase gave his assistant a few more details. 'Baxter is at the Salamanca Theater on Geary. There's a touring company doing a revival of some Broadway melodrama of a few years back. Apparently the leading man failed to emerge from his dressing room for the third act, and the manager called the police.'

Claire Delacroix shook her head, puzzled. She had drawn a silken scarf over her platinum hair and its tips were whipped by the night wind as their boat sped across the bay. 'Sounds to me like a medical problem more than a crime. Or maybe he's just being temperamental. You know those people in the arts.' Chase held his silence briefly, then grunted. 'So thought the manager until the door was removed from its hinges. The actor was seated before his mirror, stone dead.' There was a note of irony in his soft voice.

'And is that why we are ploughing through a pitch black night in the middle of winter?' she persisted.

'The death of Count Hunyadi is not a normal one, Delacroix.'

Now Claire Delacroix smiled. It was one of Abel Chase's habits to drop bits of information into conversations in this manner. If the listener was sufficiently alert she would pick them up. Otherwise, they would pass unnoted.

'Imre Hunyadi, the Hungarian matinée idol?'

'Or the Hungarian ham,' Chase furnished wryly. 'Impoverished petty nobility are a dime a dozen nowadays. If he was ever a count to start with.'

'This begins to sound more interesting, Abel. But what is this about a vampire that makes this a case for no less than the great Akhenaton Beelzebub Chase rather than the San Francisco Police Department?'

'Ah, your question is as ever to the point. Aside from the seemingly supernatural nature of Count Hunyadi's demise, of course. The manager of the Salamanca Theater states that Hunyadi has received a series of threats. He relayed this information to Captain Baxter, and Baxter to me.'

'Notes?'

'Notes — and worse. Captain Baxter states that a dead rodent was placed on his dressing table two nights ago. And today a copy of his obituary.'

'Why didn't he call the police and ask for protection?'

'We shall ask our questions when we reach the scene of the crime, Delacroix.'

Chase pulled the powerboat alongside a private wharf flanking the San Francisco Ferry Building. A uniformed police officer waited to catch the line when Chase tossed it to him. The darkly garbed Chase and the silver-clad Claire Delacroix climbed to the planking and thence into a closed police cruiser. A few snowflakes had settled upon their shoulders. Gong sounding, the cruiser pulled away and headed up Market Street, thence to Geary and the Salamanca Theater, where Chase and Delacroix alighted.

They were confronted by a mob of well-dressed San Franciscans bustling from the theater. The play had ended and, as with the younger crowd in Berkeley, the theatergoers grinned and exclaimed in surprise at the falling flakes. Few of the men and women, discussing their evening's entertainment, hailing passing cabs or heading to nearby restaurants for post-theatrical suppers, took note of the two so-late arrivers.

A uniformed patrolman saluted Abel Chase and invited him and Claire Delacroix into the Salamanca. 'Captain Baxter sends his respects, Doctor.'

'Nice to see you, Officer Murray. How are your twins? No problems with croup this winter?'

Flustered, the officer managed to stammer, 'No, sir, no problems this year. But how did you — ?'

Before Murray could finish his question he was interrupted by a stocky, ruddy-complexioned individual in the elaborate uniform of a high-ranking police officer. The Captain strode forward, visibly favoring one leg. He was accompanied by a sallow-faced individual wearing a black tuxedo of almost new appearance.

'Major Chase,' the uniformed police official saluted.

Chase smiled and extended his own hand, which the Captain shook. 'Clel. You know Miss Delacroix, of course.'

Claire Delacroix extended her hand and Captain Cleland Baxter shook it, lightly and briefly.

'And this is Mr. . . . Quince. Mr. . . . Walter Quince, wasn't it, sir?'

Walter Quince extended his own hand to Chase, tilting his torso at a slight angle as he did so. The movement brought his hatless, brilliantined head close to Chase, who detected a cloying cosmetic scent. He shook Quince's hand, then addressed himself to Baxter.

'Take me to the scene of the incident.'

Baxter led Chase and Delacroix through the now-darkened Salamanca Theater. Quince ran ahead and held aside a dark-colored velvet curtain, opening the way for them into a narrow, dingy corridor. Abel Chase and Claire Delacroix followed Baxter into the passage, followed by Quince.

Shortly they stood outside a plain door. Another police officer, this one with sergeant's chevrons conspicuous on his uniform sleeve, stood guard.

'Hello, Costello,' Chase said. 'How are

your daughter, and her husband doing these days?'

'Doctor.' The uniformed sergeant lifted a finger to the bill of his uniform cap. 'They've moved in with the missus and me. Times are hard, sir.'

Chase nodded sympathetically.

'This is Count Hunyadi's dressing room,' Quince explained, indicating the doorway behind Costello.

'I see that the door was removed from its hinges, and that Captain Baxter's men have sealed the room. That is good,' Chase noted. 'But why was it necessary to remove the hinges to open the door?'

'Locked, sir.'

'Don't you have a key, man?'

'Count Hunyadi insisted on placing a padlock inside his dressing room. He was very emphatic about his privacy. No one was allowed in, even to clean, except under his direct supervision.'

Abel Chase consulted a gold-framed hexagonal wristwatch. 'At what time was the third act to start?'

'At 10:15, sir.'

'And when was Hunyadi called?'

'He got a five-minute and a two-minute call. He didn't respond to either. I personally tried to summon him at curtain time but there was still no response.'

Abel Chase frowned. 'Did you then cancel the rest of the performance?'

'No, sir. Elbert Garrison, the director, ordered Mr. Hunyadi's understudy to go on in Mr. Hunyadi's place.'

'And who was that fortunate individual?'

'Mr. Winkle. Joseph Winkle. He plays the madman, Renfield. And Philo Jenkins, who plays a guard at the madhouse, became Renfield. It was my duty to take the stage and announce the changes. I made no mention of Count Hunyadi's — illness. I merely gave the names of the understudies.'

'Very well. Before we proceed to examine the victim and his surroundings, I will need to see these so-called threatening notes.'

Captain Cleland Baxter cleared his throat. 'Looks as if the Count was pretty upset by the notes. Everybody says he destroyed 'em all. He complained every time he got one but then he'd set a match to it.'

An angry expression swept across Chase's features.

Baxter held up a hand placatingly. 'But the latest — looks like the Count just received it tonight, Major — looks like he got riled up and crumpled the thing and threw it in the corner.'

Baxter reached into his uniform pocket and extracted a creased rectangle of cheap newsprint. 'Here it is, sir.'

Chase accepted the paper, studied it while the others stood silently, then returned it to the uniformed captain with an admonition to preserve it as potentially important evidence.

Next, he removed the police seal from the entrance to the dressing room and stepped inside, followed by Claire Delacroix, Captain Baxter, and the theater manager, Walter Quince.

Chase stood over the still form of Imre Hunyadi, for the moment touching nothing. The victim sat on a low stool, his back to the room. The head was slumped forward and to one side, the forehead pressed against a rectangular mirror surrounded by small electrical bulbs. His hands rested against the mirror as well, one to either side of his head, his elbows propped on the table.

'We observe,' Chase stated, 'that the victim is fully dressed in formal theatrical costume, complete with collar and gloves.'

'And ye'll note that he's deathly pale, Major,' the police Captain put in. 'Deathly pale. Drained by the bite of a vampire, I say.'

Chase pursed his lips and stroked his dark moustache. 'I would not be so quick to infer as much, Captain,' he warned. 'The victim's face is indeed deathly pale. That may be stage makeup, however.'

Chase lifted an emery board from the dressing table and carefully removed a speck of makeup from Hunyadi's cheek. 'Remarkable,' he commented. 'You see — ' He turned and exhibited the emery board to the room. 'It is indeed pale makeup, appropriate, of course, to the Count's stage persona. But now, we observe the flesh beneath.'

He bent to peer at the skin he had exposed. 'Remarkable,' he said again. 'As white as death.'

'Just so!' exclaimed the Captain of homicide. 'But now let us examine the victim's hands.' With great care he peeled back one of Hunyadi's gloves.

'Yet again remarkable,' Abel Chase commented. 'The hands are also white and bloodless. Well indeed, there remains yet one more cursory examination to be made.'

Carefully tugging his trousers to avoid bagging the knees of his woolen suit, he knelt beside Count Hunyadi. He lifted Hunyadi's trouser cuff and peeled down a silken lisle stocking. Then he sprang back to his full height.

'Behold!'

The Count's ankle was purple and swollen. 'Perhaps Miss Delacroix — Doctor Delacroix, I should say, will have an explanation.'

Claire Delacroix knelt, examined the dead man's ankles, then rose to her own feet and stated, 'Simple. And natural. This man died where he sits. His body was upright, even his hands were raised. His blood drained to the lower parts of his body, causing the swelling and discoloration of the ankles and feet. There is nothing supernatural about post-mortem lividity.'

Chase nodded. 'Thank you.'

He turned from the body and pointed a carefully manicured finger at Quince. 'Is there any other means of access to Hunyadi's dressing room?'

'Just the window, sir.'

'Just the window, sir?' Abel Chase's eyes grew wide. 'Just the window? Baxter — ' He turned to the Captain of police. 'Have you ordered that checked?'

Flustered, Baxter admitted that he had not.

'Quickly, then. Quince, lead the way!'

The manager led them farther along the dingy corridor. It was dimly illumined by yellow electrical bulbs. They exited through the stage door and found themselves gazing upon a narrow alley flanked by dark walls of ageing, grime-encrusted brick. To their right, the alley opened onto the normally busy sidewalk, now free of pedestrians as San Franciscans sought cover from the chill and moisture of the night. To the left, the alley abutted a brick wall, featureless save for the accumulated grime of decades.

'There it is, sir.'

Chase raised his hand warningly. 'Before we proceed, let us first examine the alley itself,' Chase instructed. Using electric torches for illumination, they scanned the thin coating of snow that covered the litter-strewn surface of the alley. 'You will notice,' Chase announced, 'that the snow is undisturbed. Nature herself has become our ally in this work.'

Chase then stepped carefully forward and turned, surveying the window. 'Fetch me a ladder,' he ordered. When the implement arrived he climbed it carefully, having donned his gloves once again. He stood peering through a narrow opening, perhaps fourteen inches wide by six inches in height. A pane of pebbled glass, mounted on a horizontal hinge in such a manner as to divide the opening in half, was tilted at a slight angle. Through it, Chase peered into the room in which he and the others had stood moments earlier.

From his elevated position he scanned the room meticulously, dividing it mentally into a geometrical grid and studying each segment in turn. When satisfied, he returned to the ground.

Walter Quince, incongruous in his evening costume, folded the ladder. 'But you see, sir, the window is much too small for a man to pass through.'

'Or even a child,' Chase added.

There was a moment of silence, during which a wisp of San Francisco's legendary fog descended icily from the winter sky. The rare snowfall, the city's first in decades, had ended. Then a modulated feminine voice broke the stillness of the tableau.

'Not too small for a bat.'

They returned to the theater. Once again inside the building, Chase doffed his warm outer coat and gloves, then made his way to the late Count Hunyadi's dressing room, where the cadaver of the émigré actor remained, slowly stiffening, before the glaring lights and reflective face of his makeup mirror. Irony tingeing his voice, Chase purred, 'You will note that the late Count casts a distinct reflection in his looking glass. Hardly proper conduct for one of the undead.' He bent to examine the cadaver once more, peering first at one side of Hunyadi's neck, then at the other.

Chase whirled. 'Was he left-handed?'

Walter Quince, standing uneasily in the doorway, swallowed audibly. 'I — I think so. He, ah, remarked something about it, I recall.'

Abel Chase placed the heels of his hands on the sides of Hunyadi's head and moved it carefully to an upright position. He made a self-satisfied sound. 'There is some stiffness here, but as yet very little. He is recently dead. Delacroix, look at this. Clel, you also.'

As they obeyed he lowered Hunyadi's head carefully to his right shoulder, exposing the left side of his neck to view above the high, stiff collar of his costume shirt.

'What do you see?' Chase demanded.

'Two red marks.' Captain Cleland

Baxter, having moved forward in his rolling, uneven gait, now leaned over to study the unmoving Hunyadi's neck. 'He played a vampire,' the police captain muttered, 'and he carries the marks of the vampire. Good God! In this Year of Our Lord 1931 — it's impossible.'

'No, my friend. Not impossible,' Chase responded. 'Supernatural? That I doubt. But impossible? No.' He shook his head.

Claire Delacroix scanned the dressing room, her dark, intelligent eyes flashing from object to object. Sensing that the attention of the theater manager was concentrated on her, she turned her gaze on him. 'Mr. Quince, the programme for tonight's performance includes a biography of each actor, is that not correct?' When Quince nodded in the affirmative, she requested a copy and received it.

She scanned the pages, touching Abel Chase lightly on the elbow and bringing to his attention several items in the glossy booklet. Chase's dark head and Claire Delacroix's platinum tresses nearly touched as they conferred.

Chase frowned at Walter Quince. 'This

biography of Mr. Hunyadi makes no mention of a wife.'

'Imre Hunyadi is — was — unmarried at the time of . . . ' He inclined his own head toward the body.

'Yes, his demise,' Chase furnished.

Quince resumed. 'Theatrical biographies seldom mention former spouses.'

'But gossip is common within the theatrical community, is it not?'

'Yes.'

There was an uncomfortable pause. Then Quince added, 'I believe he was married twice. The first time in his native Hungary. To one Elena Kadar.'

'Yes, I have heard of her,' Chase furnished. 'A brilliant woman, sometimes called the Hungarian Madame Curie. She was engaged for some years in medical research, in the field of anesthesiology. I've read several of her papers. Apparently she treated many Habsburg soldiers who had been wounded in the Great War and was greatly moved by their suffering. Hence the direction of her experiments. She ended her life a suicide. A tragic loss.'

'Ach, Major, Major, you know everything, don't you?' Captain Baxter exclaimed.

'Not quite,' Chase demurred. Then, 'Under what circumstances, Quince, was the marriage of Madame Kadar to Count Hunyadi dissolved?'

The theater manager reddened, indicating with a minute nod of his head toward Claire Delacroix that he was reluctant to speak of the matter in the presence of a female.

'Really,' Claire Delacroix said, 'I know something of the world, Mr. Quince. Speak freely, please.'

'Very well.' The manager took a moment to compose himself. Then he said, 'Some years before the Great War, Mr. Hunyadi traveled to America as a member of a theatrical troupe. *Magyar Arte*, I believe they were called. They performed plays in their native language for audiences of immigrants. While touring, Hunyadi took up with his Hungarian leading lady. A few years later they moved to Hollywood to pursue careers in motion pictures. The woman's name was — ' He looked around furtively, then mentioned the name of a popular film actress.

'They had one of those glittering Hollywood weddings,' he added.

'With no thought of a wife still in Hungary?' Claire Delacroix inquired.

Quince shook his head.

'None. Count Hunyadi made several successful silents, but when talkies came in, well, his accent, you see . . . There are just so many roles for heavily-accented European noblemen. Word within our community was that he had become a dope fiend for a time. He was hospitalized, then released, and was hoping to revive his career with a successful stage tour.'

'Yes, there were rumors of his drug habit,' Captain Baxter put in. 'We were alerted down at the Hall of Justice.'

Abel Chase looked around. 'What of — ' He named the actress who had been Imre Hunyadi's second wife.

'When her earnings exceeded his own, Count Hunyadi spent her fortune on high living, fast companions and powerful motor cars. When she cut him off and demanded that he look for other work, he brought a lawsuit against her, which failed, but which led to a nasty divorce.'

'Tell me about the other members of the cast.'

'You're thinking that his understudy might have done him in?' Baxter asked. 'That Winkle fellow?'

'Entirely possible,' Chase admitted. 'But a premature inference, Clel. Who are the others?'

'Timothy Rodgers, Philo Jenkins,' Quince supplied. 'Estelle Miller and Jeanette Stallings, the two female leads — Lucy and Mina. And of course Samuel Pollard — Van Helsing.'

'Yes.' Abel Chase stroked his moustache thoughtfully as he examined the printed programme. 'Captain Baxter, I noticed that Sergeant Costello is here tonight. A good man. Have him conduct a search of this room. And have Officer Murray assist him. And see to it that the rest of the theater is searched as well. I shall require a thorough examination of the premises. While your men perform those tasks I shall question the male cast

27

members. Miss Delacroix will examine the females.'

Baxter said, 'Yes, Major. And — is it all right to phone for the dead wagon? Count Hunyadi has to get to the morgue, don't you know, sir.'

'Not, yet, Clel. Miss Delacroix is the possessor of a medical education. Although she seldom uses the honorific, she is entitled to be called doctor. I wish her to examine the remains before they are removed.'

'As you wish, Major.'

Chase nodded, pursing his lips. 'Delacroix, have a look before you question the women of the cast, will you. And, Quince, gather these persons, Rodgers, Pollard, Winkle, and Jennings, for me. And you'd better include the director, Garrison, as well.'

Claire Delacroix conscientiously checked Hunyadi for tell-tale signs, seeking to determine the cause of the Hungarian's death. She conducted herself with a professional calm. At length she looked up from the remains and nodded. 'It is clear that the immediate cause of Count Hunyadi's death is heart failure.' She looked from one to another of the men in the dressing room. 'The puzzle is, for what reason did his heart fail? I can find no overt cause. The death might have been natural, of course. But I will wish to examine the marks on his neck. Definitely, I will wish to examine those marks.'

'I think they're a mere theatrical affectation,' Walter Quince offered.

'That may be the case,' Claire Delacroix conceded, 'but I would not take that for granted. Then' — she addressed herself to Captain Baxter — 'I would urge you to summon the coroner's ambulance and have the remains removed for an autopsy at the earliest possible moment.'

'You can rest assured of that,' Captain Baxter promised. 'Nolan Young, the county coroner, is an old comrade of mine.'

Shortly the men Chase had named found themselves back on the stage of the Salamanca Theater. The setting held ever the ominous, musty gloom of a darkened Transylvanian crypt. All had changed from their costumes to street outfits, their dark suits blending with the dull grey of canvas flats painted to simulate funereal stone.

A further macabre note was struck by their posture, as they were seated on the prop caskets that added atmosphere to the sepulchral stage setting.

Rather than a dearth, Abel Chase found that he was confronted by a surfeit of suspects. Each actor had spent part of the evening on-stage; that was not unexpected. As the hapless Jonathan Harker, Timothy Rodgers had won the sympathy of the audience, and Abel Chase found him a pleasant enough young man, albeit shaken and withdrawn as a result of this night's tragedy.

Joseph Winkle, accustomed to playing the depraved madman Renfield, tonight had transformed himself into the elegant monster for the play's final act. Philo Jenkins, the shuffling, blustering orderly, had stepped into Winkle's shoes as Renfield. It had been a promotion for each.

Yet, Abel Chase meditated, despite Captain Baxter's earlier suggestion that

Winkle might be a suspect, he would in all likelihood be too clever to place himself under suspicion by committing so obvious a crime. Philo Jenkins was the more interesting possibility. He would have known that by murdering Hunyadi he would set in motion the sequence of events that led to his own advancement into Winkle's part as Renfield. At the bottom of the evening's billing, he had the most to gain by his promotion.

And Rodgers, it was revealed, was a local youth, an aspiring thespian in his first significant role. It appeared unlikely that he would imperil the production without discernible advantage to himself.

The director, Garrison, would have had the best opportunity to commit the crime. Unlike the other cast members, who would be in their own dressing rooms — or, for such lesser lights as Rodgers, Winkle and Jenkins, a common dressing room — between the acts of the play, Garrison might well be anywhere, conferring with cast members or the theater staff, giving performance notes, keeping tabs, in particular, on a star known to have had a problem with drugs.

'Garrison.' Abel Chase whirled on the director. 'Had Hunyadi relapsed into his old ways?'

The director, sandy-haired and tanned, wearing a brown suit and hand-painted necktie, moaned. 'I was trying to keep him off the dope, but he always managed to find something. But I think he was off it tonight. I've seen plenty of dope fiends in my time. Too many, Doctor Chase. Haven't you come across them in your own practice?'

'My degree is not in medicine,' Chase informed him. 'While Miss Delacroix holds such a degree, my own fields of expertise are by nature far more esoteric than the mundane study of organs and bones.'

'My mistake,' Garrison apologized. 'For some reason, powder bouncers seem to gravitate to the acting profession as vipers do to music. Or maybe there's something about being an actor that makes 'em take wing. They start off sniffing gin and graduate to the needle. I could tell, Mister Chase, and I think Hunyadi was okeh tonight!'

Chase fixed Garrison with a calculatedly bland expression.

Unlike the actors Winkle and Jenkins, the director lacked any obvious motive for wishing Hunyadi dead. In fact, to keep the production running successfully he would want Hunyadi functional. Still, what motive unconnected to the production might Garrison have had?

And there was Samuel Pollard. As Van Helsing, Chase knew, Pollard would have appeared with the lined face and grey locks of an aged savant, a man of five decades or even six. To Chase's surprise, the actor appeared every bit as old as the character he portrayed. His face showed the crags and scars of a sexagenarian, and his thin fringe of hair was the color of old iron.

In response to Chase's questions, Pollard revealed that he had spent the second intermission in the company of the young actress who had appeared as the character Mina, Jeanette Stallings.

'Is that so?' Chase asked blandly.

'We have — a relationship,' Pollard muttered.

Chase stared at the grizzled actor, pensively fingering his moustache. He restrained himself from echoing John Heywood's dictum that there is no fool like an old fool, instead inquiring neutrally as to the nature of the relationship between Pollard and the actress.

'It is of a personal nature.' Pollard's tone was grudging.

'Mr. Pollard, as you are probably aware, I am not a police officer, nor am I affiliated with the municipal authorities in any formal capacity. Captain Baxter merely calls upon me from time to time when faced with a puzzle of special complexity. If you choose to withhold information from me I cannot compel you to do otherwise — but if you decline to assist me, you will shortly be obliged to answer to the police or the district attorney. Now I ask you again, what is the nature of your relationship with Miss Stallings?'

Pollard clasped and unclasped his age-gnarled hands as he debated with himself. Finally he bowed his head in surrender and said, 'Very well. Doctor Chase, you are obviously too young to remember the great era of the theater, when Samuel Pollard was a name to conjure with. You never saw me as Laertes, I am certain, nor as Macbeth. I was as famous as a Barrymore or a Booth in my day. Now I am reduced to playing a European vampire hunter.'

He blew out his breath as if to dispel the mischievous imps of age.

'Like many another player in such circumstances, I have been willing to share my knowledge of the trade with eager young talents. That is the nature of my relationship with Miss Stallings.'

'In exchange for which services you received what, Mister Pollard?'

'The satisfaction of aiding a promising young performer, Doctor Chase.' And, after a period of silence, 'Plus an honorarium of very modest proportions. Even an artist, I am sure you will understand, must meet his obligations.'

Chase pondered, then asked his final question of Pollard.

'What, specifically, have you and Miss Stallings worked upon?'

'Her diction, Doctor Chase. There is none like the Bard to develop one's proper enunciation. Miss Stallings is of European origin, that is, Continental, and it was in the subtle rhythms and emphases of the English language that I instructed her.'

With this exchange Abel Chase completed his interrogation of Rodgers, Winkle, Jenkins, Pollard, and Garrison. He dismissed them, first warning them that none was absolved of suspicion, and that all were to remain in readiness to provide further assistance should it be demanded of them.

He then sought out Claire Delacroix. She was found in the office of the theater manager, Walter Quince. With her were Estelle Miller and Jeanette Stallings. Chase rapped sharply on the somewhat grimy door and admitted himself to Quince's sanctum.

The room, he noted, was cluttered with the kipple of a typical business establishment. The dominant item was a huge desk. Its scarred wooden surface was all but invisible beneath an array of folders, envelopes, scraps and piles of paper. A heavy black telephone stood near at hand. A wooden filing cabinet, obviously a stranger to the cleaner's cloth no less than to oil or polish, stood in one corner. An upright typewriter of uncertain age and origin rested upon a rickety stand of suspect condition.

Claire Delacroix sat perched on the edge of the desk, occupying one of the few spots not covered by Quince's belongings. One knee was crossed over the other, offering a glimpse of silk through a slit in the silvery material of her gown.

She looked up as Abel Chase entered the room. Chase nodded.

Claire introduced him to her companions. 'Miss Miller, Miss Stallings, Doctor Akhenaton Beelzebub Chase.'

Chase nodded to the actresses. Before another word was uttered the atmosphere of the room was pierced by the shrill clatter of the telephone on Walter Quince's desk.

Claire Delacroix lifted the receiver to her ear and held the mouthpiece before her lips, murmuring into it. She listened briefly, then spoke again. At length she thanked the caller and lowered the receiver to its cradle.

'That was Nolan Young, the coroner,' she said to Chase. 'I think we had best speak in private, Abel.'

Chase dismissed the two actresses, asking them to remain on the premises for the time being. He then asked Claire Delacroix what she had learned from the county coroner.

Claire clasped her hands over her knee and studied Abel Chase's countenance before responding. Perhaps she sought a sign there of his success — or lack thereof — in his own interrogations. When she spoke, it was to paraphrase closely what Nolan Young had told her.

'The coroner's office has performed a quick and cursory postmortem examination of Imre Hunyadi. There was no visible cause of death. Nolan Young sustains my preliminary attribution of heart failure. But of course, that tells us nothing. There was no damage to the heart itself, no sign of embolism, thrombosis, or abrasion. What, then, caused Hunyadi's heart to stop beating?'

Abel Chase waited for her to continue.

'The condition of Hunyadi's irises suggests that he was using some narcotic drug, most likely cocaine.'

'Such was his history,' Chase put in. 'Nevertheless, Elbert Garrison observed Hunyadi closely and believes that he was not under the influence.'

'Perhaps not,' Claire acceded. 'An analysis of his bloodstream will tell us that. But the two marks on his neck suggest otherwise, Abel.'

Chase glanced at her sharply. He was a man of slightly more than typical stature, and she a woman of more than average height. As he stood facing her and she sat perched on the edge of Walter Quince's desk, they were eye to eye.

'Study of the two marks with an enlarging glass shows each as locus of a series of needle-pricks. I had observed as much, myself, during my own examination of the body. Most of them were old and well healed, but the most recent, Nolan Young informs, is fresh. It had apparently been inflicted only moments before Hunyadi's death. If those marks were the sign of a vampire's teeth, then the creature more likely administered cocaine to his victims than extracted blood from them.'

'You are aware, Delacroix, that I do not believe in the supernatural.'

'Not all vampires are of the supernatural variety,' she replied.

Abel Chase ran a finger pensively beneath his moustache. 'What is your professional opinion, then? Are you suggesting that Hunyadi died of erythroxylon alkaloid intoxication?'

'I think not,' frowned Claire Delacroix. 'If that were the case, I'd have expected Nolan Young to report damage to the heart and none was apparent. Further, the condition of the needle-pricks is most intriguing. They suggest that Hunyadi received no injections for some time, then resumed his destructive habit just tonight. I suspect that a second substance was added to the victim's customary injection of cocaine. The drug, while elevating his spirits to a momentarily euphoric state, would have, paradoxically, lulled him into a false sense of security while the second killed him.'

'And what do you suppose that fatal second drug to have been?'

'That I do not know, Abel. But I have a very strong suspicion, based on my conversation with the ladies of the company — and on your own comments earlier this night.'

'Very well,' Chase growled, not pleased. He knew that when Claire Delacroix chose to unveil her theory she would do so, and not a moment sooner. He changed the subject. 'What did you learn from the Misses Miller and Stallings?'

'Miss Miller is a local girl. She was born in the Hayes Valley section of San Francisco, attended the University of California in Los Angeles, and returned home to pursue a career in drama. She still lives with her parents, attends church regularly, and has a devoted male admirer.'

'What's she doing in a national touring company of the vampire play, then? She would have had to audition in New York and travel from there.'

'Theater people are an itinerant lot, Abel.'

He digested that for a moment, apparently willing to accept Claire Delacroix's judgment of the ingénue. 'Her paramour would almost certainly be Timothy Rodgers, then.'

'Indeed. I am impressed.'

'Rodgers did not strike me as a likely suspect,' Chase stated.

'Nor Miss Miller, me.'

'What about Miss Stallings?' he queried.

'A very different story, there. First of all, her name isn't really Jeanette Stallings.'

'The *nom de théâtre* is a commonplace, Delacroix. Continue.'

'Nor was she born in this country.'

'That, too, I had already learned. That was why Pollard was coaching her in diction. Where was Miss Stallings born, Delacroix, and what is her real name?'

It was the habit of neither Abel Chase nor Claire Delacroix to use a notebook in their interrogations. Both prided them-selves on their ability to retain mentally everything said in their presence. Without hesitation Claire stated, 'She was born in Szeged, Hungary. The name under which she entered the United States was Mitzi Kadar.'

'Mitzi Kadar! Imre Hunyadi's Hungar-ian wife was Elena Kadar.'

'And Mitzi's mother was Elena Kadar.'

'Great glowing Geryon!' It was as close to an expletive as Abel Chase was known to come in everyday speech. 'Was Jeanette Stallings Imre Hunyadi's daughter? There was no mention of a child in any biographical material on Hunyadi.'

'Such is my suspicion,' Claire Delacroix asserted.

'You did not have the advantage of reading the threatening note that Captain Baxter found in Hunyadi's dressing room, Delacroix.'

'No,' she conceded. 'I am sure you will enlighten me as to its content.'

'It was made up to look like a newspaper clipping,' Chase informed. 'But I turned it over and found that the obverse was blank. It appeared, thus, to be a printer's proof rather than an actual cutting. Every newspaper maintains obituaries of prominent figures, ready for use in case of their demise. When the time comes, they need merely fill in the date and details of death, and they're ready to go to press. But I don't think this was a real newspaper proof. There was no identification of the paper — was it the *Call* or the *Bulletin*, the *Tribune* or the *Gazette*? The proof should indicate.'

Abel Chase paused to run a finger beneath his moustache before resuming. 'The typographic styles of our local dailies differ from one another in subtle but significant detail. The *faux* obituary came from none of them. It was a hoax, created by a malefactor and executed by a local job printer. It was cleverly intended as a psychological attack on Hunyadi, just as was the dead rodent that was found in his dressing room.'

'And for what purpose was this hoax perpetrated?' Delacroix prompted.

'It did not read like a normal newspaper obituary,' Abel Chase responded. 'There is none of the usual respectful tone. It stated, instead, that Hunyadi abandoned his wife in Hungary when she was heavy with child.'

'An act of treachery, do you not agree?' Claire put in.

'And that his wife continued her career as a medical researcher while raising her fatherless child until, the child having reached her majority, the mother, despondent, took her own life.'

'Raising the child was an act of courage and of strength, was it not? But the crime of suicide — to have carried her grief and rage for two decades, only to yield in the end to despair — who was more guilty, the self-killer or the foul husband who abandoned her?'

Chase rubbed his moustache with the knuckles of one finger.

'We need to speak with Miss Stallings.'

'First, perhaps we had best talk with Captain Baxter and his men. We should determine what Sergeant Costello and Officer Murray have found in their examination of the premises.'

'Not a bad idea,' Chase assented,

'although I expect they would have notified me if anything significant had been found.'

Together they sought the uniformed police captain and sergeant. Costello's statement was less than helpful. He had examined the inner sill opening upon the window through which Abel Chase had peered approximately an hour before. It was heavily laden with dust, he reported, indicating that even had a contortionist been able to squeeze through its narrow opening, no one had actually done so.

'But a bat might have flown through that window, sir, without disturbing the dust,' the credulous Costello concluded.

Murray had gone over the rest of the backstage area, and the two policemen had examined the auditorium and lobby together without finding any useful clues.

'We are now faced with a dilemma,' Abel Chase announced, raising his forefinger for emphasis. 'Count Hunyadi was found dead in his dressing room, the door securely locked from the inside. It is true that he died of heart failure, but what caused his heart to fail? My assistant, Doctor Delacroix, suggests a mysterious drug administered along with a dose of cocaine, through one of the marks on the victim's neck.' He pressed two fingers dramatically into the side of his own neck, simulating Hunyadi's stigmata.

'The problem with this is that no hypodermic syringe was found in the dressing room. Hunyadi might have thrown a syringe through the small open window letting upon the alley. But we searched the alley and it was not found. It might have been retrieved by a confederate, but the lack of footprints in the so-unusual snow eliminates that possibility. A simpler explanation must be sought.'

Abel Chase paused to look around the room at the others, then resumed. 'We might accept Sergeant Costello's notion that a vampire entered the room unobtrusively, in human form. He administered the fatal drug, then exited by flying through the window, first having taken the shape of a bat. It might be possible for the flying mammal to carry an empty hypodermic syringe in its mouth. This not only solves the problem of the window's narrow opening, but that of the undisturbed dust on the sill and the untrammeled snow in the alley. But while I try to keep an open mind at all times, I fear it would take a lot of convincing to get me to believe in a creature endowed with such fantastic abilities.'

Accompanied by Claire Delacroix, Chase next met with Jeanette Stallings, the Mina of the vampire play. Jeanette Stallings, born Mitzi Kadar, was the opposite of Claire Delacroix in coloration and in manner. Claire was tall, blonde, pale of complexion and cool of manner, and garbed in silver. Jeanette — or Mitzi — sported raven tresses surrounding a face of olive complexion, flashing black eyes, and crimson lips matched in hue by a daringly modish frock.

Even her makeup case, an everyday accoutrement for a member of her profession, and which she held tucked beneath one arm in lieu of a purse, was stylishly designed in the modern mode.

'Yes, my mother was the great Elena

Kadar,' she was quick to admit. In her agitation, the nearly flawless English diction she had learned with the assistance of Samuel Pollard became more heavily marked by a European accent. 'And that pseudo-Count Hunyadi was my father. I was raised to hate and despise him, and my mother taught me well. I celebrate his death!'

Abel Chase's visage was marked with melancholy. 'Miss Stallings, your feelings are your own, but they do not justify murder. I fear that you will pay a severe penalty for your deed. The traditional reluctance of the State to inflict capital punishment upon women will in all likelihood save you from the noose, but a life behind bars would not be pleasant.'

'That remains to be seen,' Jeanette Stallings uttered defiantly. 'But even if I am convicted, I will have no regrets.'

A small sigh escaped Chase's lips. 'You might have a chance after all. From what I've heard of the late Count Hunyadi, there will be little sympathy for the deceased or outrage at his murder. And if you were taught from the cradle to regard him with such hatred, a good lawyer might play upon a jury's sympathies and win you a lesser conviction and a suspended sentence, if not an outright acquittal.'

'I told you,' Jeanette Stallings replied, 'I don't care. He didn't know I was his daughter. He pursued the female members of the company like a bull turned loose in a pasture full of heifers. He was an uncaring beast. The world is better off without him.'

At this, Chase nodded sympathetically. At the same time, however, he remained puzzled regarding the cause of Hunyadi's heart failure and the means by which it had been brought about. He began to utter a peroration on this twin puzzle.

At this moment Claire Delacroix saw fit to extract a compact from her own metallic purse. To the surprise of Abel Chase, for until now she had seemed absorbed in the investigation at hand, she appeared to lose all interest in the proceedings. Instead she turned her back on Chase and Jeanette Stallings and addressed her attention to examining the condition of her flawlessly arranged hair, her lightly rouged cheeks and pale mouth. She removed a lipstick from her purse and proceeded to perfect the coloring of her lips.

To Abel Chase's further consternation, she turned back to face the others, pressing the soft, waxy lipstick clumsily to her mouth. The stick of waxy pigment broke, smearing her cheek and creating a long false scar across her pale cheek.

With a cry of grief and rage she flung the offending lipstick across the room. 'Now look what I've done!' she exclaimed. 'You'll lend me yours, Mitzi, I know it. As woman to woman, you can't let me down!'

Before Jeanette Stallings could react, Claire Delacroix had seized the actress's makeup case and yanked it from her grasp.

Jeanette Stallings leaped to retrieve the case, but Abel Chase caught her from behind and held her, struggling, by both her elbows. The woman writhed futilely, attempting to escape Chase's grasp, screeching curses all the while in her native tongue.

Claire Delacroix tossed aside her own purse and with competent fingers opened Jeanette Stallings' makeup case. She removed from it a small kit and opened this to reveal a hypodermic syringe and a row of fluid-filled ampoules. All were of a uniform size and configuration, and the contents of each was a clear, watery-looking liquid, save for one. This container was smaller than the others, oblong in shape, and of an opaque composition.

She held the syringe upright and pressed its lever, raising a single drop of slightly yellowish liquid from its point.

'A powerful solution of cocaine, I would suggest,' Claire ground between clenched teeth. 'So Imre Hunyadi behaved toward the women of the company as would a bull in a pasture? And I suppose you ministered to his needs with this syringe, eh? A quick way of getting the drug into his bloodstream. But what is in this other ampoule, Miss Kadar?'

The Hungarian-born actress laughed

bitterly. 'You'll never know. You can send it to a laboratory and they'll have no chance whatever to analyze the compound.'

'You're probably right in that regard,' Claire conceded. 'But there will be no need for that. Anyone who knows your mother's pioneering work in anesthesiology would be aware that she was studying the so-called spinal anesthetic. It is years from practical usage, but in experiments it has succeeded in temporarily deadening all nerve activity in the body below the point in the spinal cord where it is administered.'

Jeanette Stallings snarled.

'The danger lies in the careful placement of the needle,' Claire Delacroix continued calmly. 'For the chemical that blocks all sensation of pain from rising to the brain, also cancels commands from the brain to the body. If the anesthetic is administered to the spinal cord above the heart and lungs, they shortly cease to function. There is no damage to the organs — they simply come to a halt. The anesthetic can be administered in larger or smaller doses, of course. Mixed with a solution of cocaine, it might take several minutes to work.'

To Abel Chase she said, 'In a moment, I will fetch Captain Baxter and tell him that you are holding the killer for his disposition.'

Then she said, 'You visited your father in his dressing room between the second and third acts of the vampire play. You offered him cocaine. You knew of his habit and you even volunteered to administer the dose for him. He would not have recognized you as his daughter as he had never met you other than as Jeanette Stallings. You injected the drug and left the room. Before the spinal anesthetic could work its deadly affects, Count Hunyadi locked the door behind you. He then sat at his dressing table and quietly expired.'

Still holding the hypodermic syringe before her, Claire Delacroix started for the door. Before she bad taken two steps, Jeanette Stallings tore loose from the grasp of Abel Chase and threw herself bodily at the other woman.

Claire Delacroix flinched away, holding the needle beyond Jeanette Stallings' outstretched hands. Abel Chase clutched Stallings to his chest.

'Don't be a fool,' he hissed. 'Delacroix, quickly, fetch Baxter and his men while I detain this misguided child.'

Once his associate had departed, Abel Chase released Mitzi Kadar, stationing himself with his back to the room's sole exit.

Her eyes blazing, the Hungarian-born actress hissed, 'Kill me now, if you must. Else let me have my needle and chemicals for one moment and I will end my life myself!'

Without awaiting an answer, she hurled herself at Abel Chase, fingernails extended liked the claws of an angry tigress to rip the eyes from his head.

'No,' Chase negatived, catching her once again by both wrists. He had made a lightning-like assessment of the young woman and reached his decision. 'Listen to me, Mitzi. Your deed is not forgivable but it is understandable, a fine but vital distinction. You can be saved. You had better have me as a friend than an enemy.'

As suddenly as she had lunged at the amateur sleuth, Mitzi Kadar collapsed in a heap at his feet, her hands slipping from his grasp, her supple frame wracked with sobs. 'I lived that he might die,' she gasped. 'I do not care what happens to me now.'

Abel Chase placed a hand gently on her dark hair. 'Poor child,' he murmured, 'poor, poor child. I will do what I can to help you. I will do all that I can.'

2

The Case of the Absent Aviatrix

Claire Delacroix sat cross-legged on a silken cushion, her hair piled upon her head and her face whitened and painted in the Japanese style. She wore a crimson *kimono* and contrasting *obi*, *tatami* slippers and *tabi* socks. She breathed into a bamboo *shakuhachi* flute, her graceful fingers moving over the five finger-holes of the ancient instrument. The tranquil sounds of a Buddhist *shomyo*, its tones dating to the Heian period, echoed from the high-beamed ceiling of the great room.

Twenty feet away Akhenaton Beelzebub Chase sat at his ornate desk, silver-filigreed Waterman in hand. The letter he was composing was addressed to Norbert Weiner, then visiting Cambridge University. *I trust you and Mrs. Weiner are enjoying your holiday with my old friend*

Godfrey Harold Hardy, to whom it was my pleasure to address a letter of introduction in your behalf. If it would not be an imposition, I have wondered if you would be willing to pose a few questions to Dr. Hardy on my behalf, concerning the work you and he have been pursuing in the field of quantum mechanics and Brownian motion.

At this moment the almost hypnotic sounds of the *shakuhachi* and the barely audible progress of Chase's pen across fine vellum were interrupted by the diffident arrival of Chase's *major domo* and man-of-all-work, Leicester Jenkins.

'A message, sir.'

Chase and Delacroix fixed Jenkins with keen attention.

'It's a Mr. Carter MacNeese. He insists that you know him, sir. He says that he must discuss a matter of the greatest urgency with you and requests that you take his call.'

Chase leaped to his feet. 'MacNeese! Of course I'll take his call. Bring the phone.' Jenkins disappeared briefly, returning with an instrument, which he placed upon Chase's desk. He knelt to plug it into a special outlet and retired.

'It's been a dozen years,' Chase spoke into the mouthpiece. 'I've followed your progress with pleasure.'

There was a silence during which Claire Delacroix studied the expressions pursuing one another across the face of her employer. Finally Chase said, 'All right, Mac, stand by. Delacroix and I will join you expeditiously.'

Without raising his voice but with the obvious certainty that he would be heard, he said, 'Jenkins, warm up the Hispano. Miss Delacroix and I will need it.' To Claire Delacroix he said, 'A fascinating case. I will require your assistance, if you please.'

Claire Delacroix had already risen to her feet.

'I do thank you for the music, Delacroix.' Chase nodded to his assistant. 'It made perfect accompaniment to this grey and fog-shrouded morning.'

Outside the tall casement windows of the great house the hills of the town of Berkeley and the buildings of the famous university where Chase lectured on occasion stretched away to the famous bay. Had the morning been clear the city that rose across the water, the Golden Gate itself, and the hills of Marin County to the north would have been visible. Instead, a cool, grey mist shrouded Chase's headquarters and home.

At Chase's suggestion, Claire Delacroix dressed snugly in woolen cap, sweater, skirt and boots. Chase himself added a camel's hair topcoat and soft hat to his own attire. 'We have a brief aquatic journey before us,' Chase said. 'To the distant Island of Alameda and the aerodrome of the Sapphire-MacNeese Corporation. You may need a suitable costume for flying this day, Delacroix.'

Jenkins had warmed up the Hispano-Suiza and maneuvered it beneath the *port cochère*, its immense engine running as smoothly as cream and its tonneau snug and comfortable. The custom radio receiver in the Hispano-Suiza was tuned to a local station broadcasting a program of Locatelli quintets; the melodious sounds of the great Italian's work echoed through the *port cochère*.

Before Chase had a chance to dismiss Jenkins, Claire Delacroix drew the man aside and engaged him in a discreet conference, their voices low and their exchange succinct. Jenkins nodded his understanding, touching Claire Delacroix's hand briefly as he did so.

Chase dismissed Jenkins with a curt wave of the hand and slid behind the Hispano's controls while Jenkins assisted Claire Delacroix as she settled herself in the passenger seat. When Chase pulled from the driveway he murmured, 'I suppose you are wondering at our choice of destination.'

Claire Delacroix smiled, her eyes fixed on the mist-shrouded greenery that flanked the long driveway leading from Chase's neo-Tudor manor house to the public roadway. 'Not a bit, Dr. Chase. I've seen pictures of the facility and some Sapphire-MacNeese aircraft in the Sunday rotogravure.'

Chase emitted a suggestion of a chuckle. 'Very good, very good, Delacroix. You know then that Carter MacNeese and Andrew

Sapphire are the owners of the company. Surely you are wondering why Carter Mac-Neese felt so urgent a need to communicate with me, and why we are responding to his telephone call.'

'Once again,' Claire Delacroix replied coolly, 'I'm sure you'll tell me what you wish me to know. I don't flatter myself that you asked me along purely for the pleasure of my company.'

'Carter MacNeese is a very dear friend. I have been in touch with him by mail in recent years but I have not had the pleasure of seeing him. I knew him in France and England during the Great War. He was a volunteer in the Lafayette Escadrille under French officers. Then he switched to our own air service once the United States entered the war. He flew in the 104th Aero Squadron. Said he picked it because he liked their emblem, a winged sphinx. Then the 94th. He was wingman to Eddie Rickenbacker, shot down a dozen Fokkers and Rumplers. He brought down a bombardment Zeppelin single-handed.'

The Hispano-Suiza swung onto the

main road leading toward the Oakland Estuary and the dock where they could take the ferry to Alameda.

'His luck ran out when the German ace Rudolf Berthold caught him in his sights. Mac was flying a Nieuport over Belgium; Berthold was in a Pfalz DIII when he brought him down. Mac survived the crash, not many pilots did, but it cost him a leg and an eye. Berthold sought him out after the Armistice and they became friends until Berthold was caught back on German territory by a Bolshevist gang. They strangled him with the neck ribbon of his own Blue Max.'

'Horrible!'

'When Mac recovered from his injuries he vowed that America would never be caught without a fleet of modern machines ready to take to the air. He got together with Andrew Sapphire and they started their company.'

The warehouses and piers of Oakland passed beside the Hispano-Suiza. The buildings of San Francisco were hidden by the fog that covered the bay.

'All very intriguing,' Claire Delacroix

said, 'but what has it to do with our errand today?'

'I don't know,' Chase admitted. 'Mac is an old comrade. He phoned and said that he needed my help. I have not seen him since the Great War ended although he and his partner have consulted me professionally from time to time. You may have seen blueprints and sketches of aircraft on my desk.'

'I have.'

'You have never been in a war, Delacroix, and God willing you never shall be. It's no place for a woman, and I will tell you that it's a very dangerous and unpleasant place for a man. But when an old comrade in arms calls for help, you do not hesitate, you get to his side and you provide that help. Carter MacNeese has called. I have responded.'

He shook his head, regaining his train of thought.

'Those blueprints and sketches were from Sapphire-MacNeese. We spent time in Staffordshire together, recovering from our wounds in '17 and '18. I suppose that was where the partnership was formed, although Sapphire was not Sapphire then.'

While they spoke, Abel Chase guided the Hispano-Suiza onto the automobile deck of the ferry and that craft was now crossing the estuary to the island city of Alameda. Chase and Claire Delacroix had left the great automobile and stood at the ferry's railing. The sun was powerful and its rays were beginning to burn away the fog. A brisk breeze whipped spray off the bay and misted the passengers on deck.

It was not necessary for Claire Delacroix to prompt Abel Chase. It was obvious that the telephone call from Carter MacNeese had brought vivid memories and powerful emotions flooding back to Chase.

'Back there in hospital in Staffordshire he was Aaron Saperstein. A Jewish lad from New Jersey, as I recall. The military was not very receptive to persons of his ilk, but he was a brilliant flier and he had made his way via Canada, just as I had, in order to get into the war before the Huns sent their infamous Zimmermann

Telegram and provoked Wilson into long-overdue action. Saperstein wound up in the Royal Flying Corps, then transferred to the American Air Service once our nation got into the fray.'

Claire Delacroix looked into Chase's face. He was a broad-shouldered man of above average height and she a slim, willowy woman taller than most members of her sex. There at the ferry's rail they stood eye to eye, her face raised to the level of his by spike heels, and she read in her employer's expression a far-away quality, as if he were reliving his experiences in the trenches of France and the hospital bed where he wound up, back in England.

'Aaron won us over.' Chase nodded, as if agreeing with his long-ago self. 'I will admit that there wasn't much sympathy for Hebrews among our gang, but he was a cheerful boy who had risen to the rank of major, itself quite an accomplishment for a Jew. He was resented for that, too. Carter MacNeese and I were captains then, you see, although I'd made colonel by the time I was mustered out.'

He paused briefly, a faraway look in his eyes, then resumed. 'Aaron never pulled rank, never asked for extra privileges. And he was an entertainer. Remarkably talented. He could play harmonica and banjo. Lord knows where he got musical instruments there in a temporary military hospital out in the English countryside, but he managed. He'd play tunes on the harmonica and everybody would sing along, or he'd sing and accompany himself on the banjo. He told jokes, he could do magic tricks, even hypnotized anyone who was willing. He said he'd been a schoolteacher before the war. He taught us all slight-of-hand, how to be hypnotists, anything we wanted to know. What an occupation for a man who became an aviator and then an aeroplane designer. What a show he put on — had us in stitches. And now he's an aeronautical engineer. An astonishing fellow.'

He shook his head. 'We'd better got rolling.'

The ferry was pulling into its slip on the island. Chase helped Claire Delacroix into the passenger seat, then slid behind the steering wheel. As soon as they could leave the ferry he put the Hispano-Suiza into gear and drove off the deck and onto the roadway. In minutes they were at the gate of a private airfield. Chase identified himself to the uniformed guard and they proceeded to a hangar.

On a flagpole atop the building an American flag rippled in the morning breeze. Below it a blue and golden banner showed off the Sapphire-MacNeese escutcheon. A second flagpole stood beside the first; a windsock confirmed the air movement that held the flags upright.

Chase pulled the Hispano-Suiza into a parking space beside the hangar, between a LaSalle touring car and a Nash coupé. Before he and Claire Delacroix had fully exited the Hispano-Suiza, Andrew Sapphire emerged from the building and trotted to greet them.

'Mac is inside, Abel. He can't wait to see you.'

Sapphire shook hands heartily with Abel Chase. When Chase introduced Claire Delacroix, Sapphire took her proffered hand and bent over it briefly, presenting the illusion without the reality of a kiss.

He was shorter than she, with a hooked nose and thickly curled, black hair. He was casually dressed in plaid shirt, canvas trousers and boots. Claire Delacroix had never encountered such a person. He was so full of energy that he almost bounced in place even when he tried to stand still.

'Come on,' he urged. He spoke with the harsh accent and vigorous pronunciation of a denizen of an East Coast slum. 'Chase, what a treat! Come on, man. We'll open a bottle and toast the old aero days!'

Inside the hangar the air was chilly and damp. Claire Delacroix pulled her warm coat around her. Several aeroplanes stood in varying stages of repair. Nearest to the huge rolling doors were two identical aircraft of a type Claire Delacroix had never seen, sleek models with red-painted bodies and silver wings and tail empennage, but before she could learn anything about them she was ushered, along with Abel Chase, into a closed office.

Carter MacNeese limped across the

room to greet the newcomers. He had the red hair and freckled complexion of a boisterous Irish youth, but the lines in his face and pain in his one eye that showed even in a moment of happy reunion were those of a older and sadder man. He might have recovered from the injuries that the German Berthold inflicted, but he would never get back the eye or the leg that he lost in their violent aerial encounter.

'A joy to see you, Abel! And this must be the wondrous Miss Delacroix you've told me of so often.' He took both Claire's hands in his own, balancing on his good leg and the artificial replacement of the one he had lost. 'And I must introduce Miss — '

The room was furnished with two wooden desks, one obviously belonging to MacNeese, the other to Sapphire. The chill in the air was relieved somewhat by an electric heater that glowed orange between the desks. In addition to the desks and the wooden chairs that stood behind them, a battered overstuffed sofa and matching leather-covered easy chair completed the creature comforts of the room. The walls were decked with pictorial calendars for the present year, 1931, and with heroic prints of aviators and their aircraft, from the hot air balloons of the eighteenth century to the sleek fighting ships and passenger-carriers of the present.

A glassed window permitted occupants of the office to watch activities in the hangar proper, where mechanics were working on a variety of aeroplanes.

'I'm Eleanor Lown,' the woman who had interrupted MacNeese introduced herself.

'I've heard of your exploits,' Claire Delacroix responded. They exchanged a handshake.

Eleanor Lown's hands were long and graceful, more like Claire Delacroix's than the mannish hands she might have expected. 'You are a credit to womankind, Miss Lown.'

'Eleanor.'

'Claire.'

It was as quick and simple, yet as subtle, as that. A bond was formed.

Carter MacNeese limped back to his desk. The desk was as battered and as functional as the sofa and the easy chair from which Eleanor Lown had risen. MacNeese opened a drawer and lifted a bottle from it. In minutes everyone in the room — MacNeese, Sapphire, Lown, Chase, Delacroix — was holding a chipped coffee mug not filled with coffee.

'Bottled in bond prewar *schnapps*,' MacNeese announced.

His partner, Sapphire, raised his coffee mug. 'To Kaiser Bill,' he toasted, 'damn his eyes and hang him to a sour apple tree!'

They drank.

MacNeese said, 'Kaiser Bill was a bad actor all right, but the way things are going there in Germany, we may wish he were still in power. Poor old Hindenburg is the last bulwark of anything resembling democracy in that country. Mark my word, once the old man is gone it's going to be a scramble between the Bolshies and the Nazis to see who grabs the reins, and whichever one it is we'll wish it was the other.'

'A grim note,' Abel Chase stated. 'But we have a more immediate concern, have we not? When you sounded the alarm, Mac, Delacroix and I responded. I would expect no less of any old comrade. But you didn't summon us just to defy the Volstead Act and reminisce about the Great War. What's the great emergency.'

'All right.' MacNeese took another draught from his mug, then settled it on his desktop and himself in his wooden chair. 'Did you notice the two red and silver aeroplanes in the hangar as you came in, Abel?'

Claire Delacroix watched as Abel Chase nodded his positive.

'Recognize anything?' MacNeese fixed Chase with a keen gaze from his single eye. The cavity whence he had lost the other was covered by a black patch that gave him a piratical look.

'Of course.' Chase nodded. 'I vetted those plans for you six months ago. They were almost flawless. The monocoque fuselage and cantilever wing surely represent the future of high-performance aircraft.'

'A far cry from the cloth-covered wooden skeletons that Andrew and I flew in the war,'

MacNeese grinned.

'We used to watch them going over,' Chase said. 'Sometimes, down in the trenches, we envied you fliers your comfortable lives. Out on a mission, home to a warm, clean bed.'

'Yes,' Sapphire added. 'And a cold pint, a hot meal, and occasionally a warm *mam'selle* to help us celebrate the memories of fallen comrades.' He lifted his coffee cup and took a healthy swig. 'I hope the ladies present will forgive me for that remark.'

Eleanor Lown laughed. 'Forgiven,' she grinned. 'And I doubt that Claire is dreadfully shocked. Are you, Claire?'

Before Claire Delacroix could reply, MacNeese banged his empty mug on his desktop.

'Enough social palaver. Abel, you're getting impatient to know what this is about. I'll tell you. In a few minutes I expect you'll want to inspect the two SM-9's in the hangar. You know how I feel about the future of warfare. I don't like it any more than the next man, any more than anyone who's ever seen what war does.'

'I know what it cost you, Mac. There were days in Staffordshire when I wondered if you were going to make it. And if you did, whether you'd curse God for not calling you home instead of sending you back to the world with your losses.'

'I don't like war,' MacNeese repeated, 'but there's another one coming. I can feel it in my bones. I can see it more clearly with the one eye I have left than ever I saw anything when I had two. If the Bolshies get Germany, Poland will be gone in a week. Comrade Stalin is going to want Italy and France once he gets Germany and Poland. Then our English cousins will be shaking in their boots and before you know it there will be a war to make the last one look like a Sunday school outing.'

'And if the Bolshevists don't get Germany?' Claire Delacroix asked.

Andrew Sapphire took over. 'The only

thing that can stop the Bolshevists is the Nazis. They're as bad or worse. That thug Hitler makes my blood boil.'

'And as for Andrew,' MacNeese put in, 'Why, Hitler is out to exterminate the Jews. He won't stop, he won't even pause until he has the continent in his pocket. Then the British Isles and then — don't think that the Atlantic Ocean will protect us from his hordes.'

Sapphire bounced from his seat and paced the room, leaving his coffee mug behind, gesturing with both hands. 'The moneyed interests in Germany think Hitler will save them from Stalin, then they'll either use him as a puppet or they'll get rid of him. They think because he's crude, because he was a corporal in the Great War and they were in tight with the Junkers that Hitler is stupid. They'll learn better, mark my words. They'll learn better and the lesson they learn will be a bitter one. But it will be too late for them.'

'So you see,' MacNeese resumed, 'we're getting ready. This country is so concerned with itself, hardly anyone is looking at Europe and seeing the danger. President Hoover wants to convince us that prosperity is just around the corner. The Democrats think if we just legalize beer and tax it they can use the revenue to solve all our problems. They both make me sick. We need to pay attention to the world. If the government won't pay attention, we'll do it for them. That's why Andrew and I are developing the SM-9.'

'That ship will hit 300 miles per hour once we get the proper power-plant in it,' Sapphire asserted. 'Right now we're using 300 horsepower Wright radials but Wright is building a 500 horsepower mill and we're going to replace the ones we have now as soon as they come in. She'll have a ceiling of 15,000 feet and a range of 600 miles. She'll carry half a dozen fixed-firing machine guns and a light cannon. Plus another little surprise that you'll learn about soon. She'll knock anything the Germans have out of the sky.'

'But wait.' Claire Delacroix had been listening closely, holding her own counsel. Now she spoke up. 'The Germans don't even have a military air service. They're forbidden by treaty. All they have are passenger planes and Zeppelins.'

'I don't believe it,' Sapphire countered bitterly. 'If Hitler comes to power — or the Reds — they'll be building bombardment ships and fighters before you can blink. I don't trust them. They have some of the finest minds in the world in that country and some of the most evil men ever born. If somebody doesn't stop them — quick-time — you'll see grey uniforms parading in Paris before the end of the decade.'

'All right,' Chase said calmly. 'Your political ideas are your own. Mac — '

Sapphire cut him off. 'You don't understand, Dr. Chase. The dictators and the kings are coming back from defeat. Mussolini has Victor Emmanuel in his pocket and the Vatican under his thumb. Hitler keeps hinting that he's going to bring Wilhelm back from exile Holland, *El Rey* is sitting in Lisbon with his bags packed and his ticket back to Madrid in his pocket. Paris is crawling with Russian princes and grand dukes hoping for a

Tsarist restoration. And down in the Balkans, the tinder box of Europe, Alexander is running around like a make-believe Holy Roman Emperor. America has to — '

'Please, Andrew.' Abel Chase gestured for silence. 'Please. Europe has her problems, no doubt. But Mac telephoned me with an urgent problem this morning. Delacroix and I have traveled to Alameda to offer our assistance. You have yet to come to the point.'

MacNeese responded. 'Very well. Andrew, my leg is bothering me. Would you show Dr. Chase and Miss Delacroix the SM-9's. I'd like to hobble out there with Miss Lown, but perhaps you'll excuse us for now. It's difficult for me, you see. Abel, I'm sorry that we're roundabout. What has happened is so astounding, Andrew and I are passionate about this, as you can see.'

'I can.'

'Well, if you don't mind, look over the ships and then return. We'll await you here. When you hear what happened this morning you'll understand why we're all so disordered.'

Chase and Claire Delacroix followed Andrew Sapphire out of the office.

The SM-9's were apparently identical, save for the serial numbers painted on their wings and fuselages. They stood on their streamlined landing gear, their bodies glistening beneath the powerful lights that filled the gloom of the hangar with a simulation of bright daylight. Each ship had dual cockpits and windshields. The designs were sleek, the radial engine cylinders covered with smooth cowlings.

Chase ran his hands over the leading edge of the wing of one ship, then studied the cleanly riveted fuselage closely. There was no sign of weaponry.

Andrew Sapphire, observing Chase's reaction, said, 'They're not fitted with guns now. No need for them on these prototypes. We're trying desperately to get the War Department to take an interest, fit the ships up with armament, but they're still shell-shocked from their battle with Billy Mitchell. They don't even want to talk to us. And as for the Navy, they're still fighting the Spanish at

Guantanamo no less the Great War.'

'Why are they two-seaters?'

'That's the beauty of it, Chase! The pilot sits in the front seat and fires the wing guns and the cannon. You know the biggest peril of aerial warfare. If the enemy gets above and behind you, you haven't a prayer. We'll put a stop to that. The second crewman in the SM-9 has a set of controls and a pair of guns of his own. If someone tries to dive on a Nine from behind, he's in for a very nasty surprise.'

'All right.' Chase climbed into the cockpit of one of the ships and studied its instruments.

When he was satisfied he descended to the hangar's cement floor. 'Delacroix, have you seen what you need to see? Good. Let's get back to MacNeese and Miss Lown. Andrew, I could see that Mac is in pain. Is he always this bad?'

'Sometimes worse.'

'Poor chap. Come, then, Delacroix, let's find out what the mystery is about.'

Back in the office Chase said, 'The SM-9 looks like a fine aeroplane. I'm flattered that you incorporated the suggestions I offered when you sent me the plans, Mac.'

'We're grateful for your help, sir,' Sapphire put in.

'I noticed that the cowlings were still warm and there was carbon around the exhausts. Those ships were flown very recently.'

'Yes.'

'I also noticed several other features that intrigued me. I infer that you added them at my suggestion when I evaluated your blueprints some months ago. The second set of controls in the rear cockpit, the revolving seat that permits the second crew member to face forward as a relief pilot or rearward as a gunner. And the optical device that permits the rear crew member to scan the sky as a periscope permits a submariner to scan the ocean's surface.'

MacNeese said, 'The design changes you suggested were immensely valuable, Abel. I know the little memento that Andrew and I sent you as token of our appreciation could never repay you for your help.'

'Appreciated nonetheless, Mac. Now, Andrew, tell me what happened.'

'Miss Lown was flying an SM-9. She was in the front seat. Even though most two-seaters are normally flown from the rear seat, in the Nine the rear seat is chiefly for the gunner. As Mac told you, the ship has dual controls. She can be flown from either position but she's normally flown from the front position.'

'That I understand. You may recall whose suggestion that arrangement was, gentlemen.'

'Right. Sorry. Karol Raynor was in the rear seat. She was flying for familiarization. She's also a consultant to the aero corps of her nation.'

'And what nation is that?' Abel Chase inquired.

Andrew Sapphire said, 'The former Kingdom of the Serbs, Croats and Slovenes, now known as Jugoslavia, thanks to King Alexander. Take a look at the map and you'll see that it's nothing but the old Greater Serbia come back to haunt the Balkans. All the world needs is another Grand Duke assassinated and we go up in flames all over again.'

'Yes, yes,' his partner soothed him. 'Nevertheless, we've got a company to run, and if we can't get our own government to pay attention to our aeroplanes, maybe we can get the Jugoslavians to buy some Nines.'

'You'd think they could buy from Tony Fokker in Holland or the Short brothers in England. Or from the Russians. They've got some excellent designers, Tupolev, Antonov, Gurevich, Yakovlev, building an aero corps for them. Putting together great monoplanes and dropping soldiers with parachutes. The world had better watch out for them.'

'Yes. Well, I know Miss Lown's credentials,' Chase brought the conversation back to topic. 'She's flown in the Bendix and Thompson races, she's unquestionably the finest female test pilot in the world and probably as good as most men.'

At this, Claire Delacroix detected a faint smile crossing Eleanor Lown's features. 'But perhaps you'll tell me something about this Karol Raynor,'

Chase continued.

Now Eleanor Lown spoke. 'She's a farm girl from a little town near Zagreb. Her brother Herbert built a biplane from plans in *Scientific Experimenter* magazine, or so she told me. Once he'd built the aeroplane he had to teach himself to fly so he bought a book on that subject and sat at the controls and practiced until he was ready, then he filled the tank with fuel and took off from a pasture on their farm.'

'A remarkable achievement,' Chase commented.

Eleanor Lown's enthusiasm was obvious. 'Once Karol saw Herbert take to the air, he had no peace from her until he'd promised to teach her to fly. She was only twelve at the time, Herbert was nineteen. She had to sit on a couple of books to see through the windshield but she was an apt pupil and she was flying in a matter of days. She's wonderful. I love her.'

'No doubt.' Chase crossed the room and peered into the hangar work area. 'The two of you took off in the SM-9.

Were there any other aircraft in the vicinity?'

'I followed in the other Nine,' Sapphire put in. 'I invited Mac to come along but he elected to stay here in the shop.'

'True,' affirmed MacNeese.

'All right,' Chase said. 'Now, suppose Miss Lown tells us what happened next. Everything you can think of, Miss Lown, if you please. Sapphire, please attend closely. You may need to amplify or correct Miss Lown's narrative. Delacroix, are you paying attention? I know you refuse to take notes, I'm sure you'll retain everything that you hear.'

He had been speaking half over his shoulder as he observed activities in the hangar. Now he spun on his heel and faced into the office. 'Miss Lown, proceed!'

Eleanor Lown nodded. 'First we met with Mr. Sapphire. He talked to us about the planes and our flight. Of course I know the SM-9 like the back of my hand, I've been flying her from the beginning, but Karol didn't know the ship nearly as well as I did. I tried to pay close attention

86

to Mr. Sapphire but of course he was talking more to Karol than he was to me. I'm sorry, Mr. Sapphire, but you know, you do go on sometimes. Maybe I didn't get enough sleep last night, but I thought you were droning on.'

'I'm sorry if I bored you, Miss Lown.'

Andrew Sapphire or Aaron Saperstein, thought Abel Chase, either way, the man does not like criticism.

'Karol and I checked the ship together,' the aviatrix resumed. 'She wanted to learn everything she could about it. I let her climb into the front cockpit and study the controls. Then she transferred to the rear position and I climbed in. The Nine has a self-starter, Dr. Chase, I don't know if anyone mentioned that.'

'I am aware of the arrangement, thank you.'

'A couple of the boys rolled the Nine out onto the tarmac. I looked back, I could see Andrew in the second ship. He was alone.'

Chase shot a sharp glance at Andrew Sapphire who nodded his assent.

'The Wright radial started right up,'

Eleanor Lown said. 'It was a chilly morning but the ships had spent the night in the hangar so they weren't too cold. I checked the windsock and saw there was a brisk breeze coming off the bay. Our boys put chocks under the Nine's wheels so I could rev the radial up.'

'Good. Now,' Chase prompted, 'we know that the morning was chilly and there was a brisk breeze blowing onshore. What other weather conditions did you note?'

'There had been a heavy ground fog during the night,' Eleanor Lown said. 'I don't like to fly in soup.'

'No sensible pilot does,' Sapphire inserted.

'But the fog was lifting,' Eleanor Lown continued. 'Visibility was already fair and it was improving. I gave the thumbs-up to Andrew, and in case Carter was watching from the hangar. I revved up the Wright, gave the signal to the mechanics and they pulled the chocks, and we were off. The Nine doesn't need a long runway for takeoff. In a few minutes we were over the bay. We'd got above the fog. There were some clouds but the sun was strong, I could feel it on my face.'

'What was Miss Raynor doing during this time?' Chase asked.

'I was paying close attention to the Nine and to putting her through her paces. I was hardly aware of my passenger. It's like that when I'm flying, I'm in another realm. The Nine is a pleasure to fly. It's — almost Godlike to be up there above the earth, no buildings, no traffic, no people, just you and your ship. It's like making love.'

'Yes,' Chase said. 'Very poetic. But about Miss Raynor. Did she ask any questions? Make any comments?'

'None that I remember.'

'What about Andrew Sapphire in the second ship?'

'I saw him a couple of times while I put the Nine through her paces, flying loops and Immelmanns, banking turns, I spotted the other Nine. But I wasn't paying too much attention to the other ship. That was the plan. Karol and I were the primary. We were to set the pace. Andrew was our escort.'

'I was their wingman,' Sapphire said, 'just like over France and Belgium.'

'The aeroplane performed well?' Chase asked.

'Beautifully. She flies like a dream.'

'Please go on, then.'

'Well, I finished putting the ship through her paces. The day was getting so lovely up there — I could see there was still fog beneath me — it was tempting to set a course and just fly on. But of course that was not what we had planned. This was a business flight, not a lark, so I headed back to Alameda. Even through what was left of the fog, I could see the island clearly enough, sitting here alongside the estuary. I brought the ship in for a landing, cut the engine, and climbed out.'

The aviatrix reached for her previously abandoned coffee mug and studied its interior. Then she raised her eyes. 'I was alone.'

There was silence in the office. The sounds of mechanics at work in the hangar, the sound of voices raised in banter, the sounds of tools on metal parts, found their way into the little room.

'You were alone,' Abel Chase returned.

'Yes, sir. For a moment I hardly noticed. I guess I was in a trance. I felt that way. It wasn't anything new for me, I often find myself disoriented when I return to the ground after a very special flight.'

'I'll second that,' MacNeese offered. 'It was that way in France and Belgium. You'd come back from a mission and it was like moving from one world to another, the world of the sky to the world of the ground. Disoriented is exactly the word for it, Miss Lown.'

Chase said, 'Yes, yes, that's all very well. But what about Miss Raynor?'

'Well,' Eleanor Lown made an odd gesture with her right hand, a gesture such as a blind woman would make when reaching for a familiar object and not finding it in its accustomed place. 'Well, I just looked around. When I got reoriented I realized that I'd had a passenger on my flight. This only took a few seconds once I had my feet on the tarmac, of course. I looked around for Karol and I didn't see her. I climbed up and looked in her cockpit but she wasn't there.'

Abel Chase fixed the aviatrix with keen, heavy-lidded eyes. 'You didn't see your passenger. What *did* you see?'

'I looked around. I heard a Wright radial engine, they have a distinctive tone, you see, and I looked up and there was Mr. Sapphire just coming in for a landing in the other SM-9. I waited until he was on the ground, then I ran over and — and I'm afraid I wasn't entirely coherent.'

'All right,' said Chase. 'Thank you, Miss Lown. I think that's enough information for the moment. Now, Mr. Sapphire — you do prefer to be called Sapphire, not Saperstein, is that not so? — well, Mr. Sapphire, what's your version of this story? Do you have anything to add to Miss Lown's narrative?'

'Nope.' Sapphire scowled.

'Did you not observe Miss Lown and Miss Raynor's aeroplane as Miss Lown put it through its paces? That was your purpose in flying the second ship, was it not?'

'I saw them, all right. Eleanor is a

terrific air-jockey. I matched her, maneuver for maneuver.'

'You never lost sight of Miss Lown's aeroplane.'

'Never.'

Abel Chase stroked his chin. Again there was silence in the office and again the sounds of the busy hangar came to the conferees. Finally Chase nodded as if affirming for himself a decision. 'Miss Lown mentioned both a ground fog or mist through which she took off, and I believe some clouds. Delacroix, what was the reference?'

'Miss Lown said, 'We were over the bay. We'd got above the fog. There were some clouds but the sun was strong, I could feel it on my face'.'

'Is that correct, Miss Lown?'

'Yes.'

'Did you fly through the clouds?'

'Yes.'

'Could Mr. Sapphire have observed you at all times, even as you were flying through the clouds? I ask because I am not myself an aviator. I have traveled in several aeroplanes and in a Cierva gyroplane, but only as a passenger.'

Eleanor Lown pursed her lips as if summoning up her recollection of the flight. 'I know that ships disappear from sight when they fly through clouds, if the clouds are thick enough. Then they reappear, of course.'

'Were you watching Mr. Sapphire in the second SM-9?'

'No.' She shook her head. She had somehow located a brush and applied it to her hair, earlier crushed against her scalp by a leather flying helmet. Rich brown curls now framed her face. 'No,' she repeated, 'I wasn't paying any attention to the other ship. I have confidence in Mr. Sapphire's piloting skills. I knew he would keep a safe distance between our ships. I was concentrating on my job, on showing the SM-9 and her performance to Karol Raynor.'

'That is fair enough.' Chase strode to the window and gazed into the hangar, his hands clasped in the small of his back. He had expected the two red and silver monoplanes to have been rolled into the hangar once more, but they were not to be seen. Turning once again he faced Andrew Sapphire.

'Please think before you answer, sir. Did you not lose sight of the other ship when it plunged into the clouds, as Miss Lown states it did?'

Sapphire muttered something to himself, something inaudible to the others. Then he said, 'Yes, now that you mention it. The Nine was executing an inside loop. It rose into the cloud, it was a medium-sized cumulus, disappeared, then dived back out. I did lose sight of it for a few seconds. You don't suggest that . . . ' He stopped, not as if he were pausing for effect but as if he had simply run out of words.

'Don't suggest what?' Chase inquired.

'I don't know. Do you read those wild adventure magazines, Dr. Chase? The ones with stories about rocket ships and invisibility rays? I suppose an invisible aeroplane might have been waiting there inside the cloud, or maybe a strange aerial creature that grabbed Miss Raynor out of the SM-9 and made off with her.'

Sapphire laughed at his own absurd suggestion.

'No,' Chase shook his head. He did not crack a smile. 'This is serious business, sir. We are here to deal with the possible, however fantastic it may seem. Miss Raynor was in that ship when it went up and she was not there when it came back down. Ergo, she left the ship at some point during her flight. We must find out when and how that happened. Once we do so we will find Miss Raynor. That I can promise you. I hope we will find her alive and well, but find her we shall.'

Carter MacNeese said, 'That sounds good, Abel, but how do you propose to do it?' Chase reached inside his jacket and drew a fountain pen, a duplicate of the filigreed Waterman he habitually used at his desk, from an inside pocket. He handed it to MacNeese. 'Will you protect this for me, Mac? It was a gift from someone very important to me, whom I know I will never see again.' He paused, studying the pen, then laid it in MacNeese's outstretched hand. 'Not in this world, at any rate,' he added.

'All right!' Chase clapped his hands, drawing the focus of everyone in the office. 'Are the two SM-9's ready to fly?'

Sapphire said they were.

'Don't they need to be refueled?'

'A demonstration flight like this morning's doesn't use much fuel, Dr. Chase. There's plenty of the juice left in their tanks.'

'That being the case, I propose that we duplicate this morning's exercise. Of course conditions will not be identical. It is later in the day, the sun is higher, the fog is mostly gone, and the cloud formations are constantly shifting. Still, we must come as close as possibly we can.'

He strode to the door. 'I propose that Miss Lown take up the same ship she took this morning. Delacroix, you will play the role of Karol Raynor, occupying the rear cockpit of Miss Lown's SM-9.'

Having said that, he faced Andrew Sapphire. 'You will fly the wingman's ship, just as you did earlier today, sir. But instead of flying alone, you will have company — mine. I will occupy the rear cockpit of your aeroplane.'

Sapphire widened his eyes. 'You and Miss Delacroix are not pilots, Dr. Chase, no less test pilots.'

'Oh, Delacroix is indeed a qualified and licensed aviatrix. I have flown with her and I can testify to her great skill at the stick. As for me, you are right, I am not a qualified pilot. I will be a mere passenger and observer. I will be at your mercy, sir. I trust that arrangement is satisfactory.'

Sapphire pushed himself erect. 'As you wish, Dr. Chase. We can be off the ground and in the air before you can say Jack Robinson.'

'Miss Lown,' Chase said, 'can you retrace your course and duplicate your maneuvers of this morning?'

The aviatrix hesitated, then said, 'I think I can, Dr. Chase.'

Abel Chase offered a rare, encouraging smile. 'I'm sure you can, Miss Lown.' Minutes later they were seated in the SM-9s. Eleanor Lown kicked over the starter on their ship. With a single burst of grey exhaust the engine caught and the gracefully-formed, three-bladed propeller whirled into invisibility.

Twenty yards behind the ship and as far to its flank, the second SM-9 also roared into life. Hearing the loud cough of its engine, Claire Delacroix turned in her seat to observe the other aeroplane, Andrew Sapphire at the controls in the front cockpit and Claire's employer, Abel Chase, behind him in the relief pilot and rear gunner's cockpit.

Eleanor Lown turned and spoke over her shoulder. 'Hang on, Claire. I know you're a flier, you won't have any trouble with this. You won't mind some aerobatics, I hope.' Her voice was strong and Claire Delacroix had no trouble making out her words despite the roar of their ship's Wright radial.

The aviatrix revved the engine and signaled the mechanics. The chocks were pulled and the sleek red-and-silver machine surged ahead. Claire Delacroix felt herself pushed back into her seat. The hangars and palm trees that lined the runway raced past, turning from discrete objects into a colorful blur. Then the SM-9 lifted into the air, a true denizen of the sky freed from its temporary bondage to the solid earth.

The wind rushed past Claire Delacroix's face. She pulled down her clear goggles to protect her eyes, noting that Eleanor Lown did the same at virtually the same moment.

A thin layer of grey was all that remained of the morning's fog. Claire Delacroix felt its cool, moist touch on her cheeks. Then Eleanor Lown gave the ship its head; roaring upward in a steep, banking climb. They burst through the last of the mist into a bright day, the sky a perfect blue and the sun a brilliant, blazing disk.

There were a few clouds but they were several thousand feet above the aeroplane. 'Is this where you did that loop, Eleanor?' Claire Delacroix had to raise her voice in order to be heard.

Eleanor Lown nodded.

'Was that before or after the Immelmann?'

Eleanor Lown shouted, 'Immelmann first. I'll follow the same pattern, okeh? Here we go!'

She put the SM-9 into a near-vertical climb, banking sharply as the aeroplane rose, kicking the ship around with the ailerons and tail pedal.

Claire Delacroix felt the blood rush from her head. She experienced a moment of vertigo and spots danced before her eyes. Then the SM-9 leveled off again, the sun glinting from her silver wings and whirling propeller.

'Are you all right?' Eleanor Lown shouted over her shoulder. 'Sorry, I should have warned you about that.'

Claire Delacroix gulped refreshing mouthfuls of clear air, clearing her head at the same time. 'I'm all right, thanks. What a thrill. Imagine pilots doing that in the war, fighting for their lives.'

Claire Delacroix studied the instruments on the panel before her. The ship was cruising at more than 200 miles per hour. The altimeter read 10,000 feet — they were almost two miles above the Bay. A curved windshield deflected the worst of the slipstream but the wind still pressed its cold, moist fingers against her cheeks.

To permit the rear crewmember to function alternately as relief pilot and as rear gunner, the seat of the back cockpit was made so it could revolve. Leg room was at a premium, and Claire Delacroix's long, slim limbs were tight-pressed, but she managed to turn in the cockpit. She spotted the second SM-9 some hundred yards behind Eleanor Lown and herself. Here in its natural element the ship appeared even more graceful than it did on the ground. Graceful, yes, but powerful, too, in a potent, oddly masculine way. Armed with machine guns and cannon, the ship would be a powerful weapon of war. The nation whose forces were equipped with aeroplanes like this would make a formidable foe for any opponent.

Claire's attention was called back by Eleanor Lown's voice. 'Are you ready for the loop, Claire?'

She faced forward, grasping the stick with both hands. 'Let's go!'

Eleanor Lown gunned the Wright radial to maximum power and pulled back on her stick. The SM-9 pointed her nose at a giant cumulonimbus. As the ship roared into the cloud Claire Delacroix cast a quick look behind. There was the second SM-9 with Sapphire and Abel Chase in its cockpits, and below it the waters of San Francisco Bay, the city itself to the west and the Island of Alameda and the East Bay cities of Oakland and Berkeley beyond.

Once inside the cloud Claire Delacroix lost track of which way was up and which was down. Everything was white. Then she felt the aeroplane tilt backwards. She clutched at the stick. If she hadn't held onto it she felt that she would have tumbled head-downward out of the cockpit. She had the illusion, the fantasy that the cloud was a bed of soft material that would catch her and lower her gently toward the water below, but she fought down a momentary impulse to let go of the stick and float away.

She knew the reality, that if she let go she would fall straight down for — how high above the surface was the ship? When last she'd checked the altimeter they were at 10,000 feet and still climbing. They were two miles above the earth. The air was cold and wet and getting thin. There was a ringing in her ears. She inhaled as deeply as she could.

She felt the seat pressing upward against her. With a roar the aeroplane burst out of the cloud-bottom and leveled off. Claire Delacroix felt as she had when she was ten years old and a group of schoolgirls, herself included, had first ridden the roller-coaster at Crown Beach in Alameda. The combination of terror and exhilaration had made an impression that was stored deep within in her brain, that came to the surface at moments like this. She hoped that Eleanor Lown intended to settle for a single loop-the-loop. She didn't know if she could survive another.

But she knew now what had happened to Karol Raynor. She knew, or at least she had a strong hunch. She had a notion that she knew what had happened to the foreign aviatrix but she did not know how it had happened, or why.

She swung around in her seat and saw the second SM-9, with Andrew Sapphire at the controls and Abel Chase in the second cockpit, emerge from the bottom of the fluffy cumulus cloud. She scanned the sky above and below the aeroplane. From the corner of her eye she caught sight of another aircraft flying below them. It was a Cierva gyroplane.

She blinked, realizing that it was the identical craft that she herself had flown on occasion. Leicester Jenkins, then, must be at the controls. Surprisingly, Jenkins had folded the rotary blades that gave the aircraft most of its lift. Flying only on the strength of its propeller and lifted only by its stubby wings, the gyroplane was steadily losing altitude.

To Claire Delacroix's startlement, Eleanor Lown let out a sudden exclamation, half howl and half yelp, and pointed toward the cloud. A black speck was silhouetted against it. The speck resolved itself into a human figure, at first tumbling, then righting itself, arms and legs spread to provide maximum drag and slow its fall. Still, the figure accelerated downward.

With a thump that Claire Delacroix

could hear, either in actuality or in her imagination, the falling man crashed onto one of the gyroplane's stubby wings. The gyroplane staggered in midair as a boxer would stagger when he received a massive body-blow. Chase clung there, then slowly and painfully pulled himself to the fuselage. Leicester Jenkins reached over the side of the rocking gyroplane and half-dragged, half-helped the other man into the passenger seat of the Cierva.

Then Claire Delacroix saw Jenkins lean over the controls. In seconds the locked overhead rotors began once more to windmill and the Cierva gyroplane gained altitude. It swung around, heading back toward the Island of Alameda and the Sapphire-MacNeese installation.

Astonished, Claire Delacroix regained control of herself and leaned forward. She reached around the windshield, grasping Eleanor Lown by the shoulder. She found herself wishing she'd worn gloves. She'd flown before, not only conventional aeroplanes but the Cierva gyroplane that the brilliant Spanish inventor had shipped to Oakland for Abel Chase's examination and evaluation, and had deeded to Chase in gratitude for the latter's keenly analytical report, but she was not accustomed to flying in an open-cockpit ship at this altitude.

'Eleanor,' she shouted, 'Eleanor.'

The pilot turned in her seat. Even through their goggles, Claire Delacroix detected an odd glaze in Eleanor Lown's eyes.

'Eleanor, pay attention!' she shouted.

The aviatrix shook her head violently, as one does to shake the cobwebs out of one's brain.

'What is it?'

'Are you all right, Eleanor?'

Eleanor Lown blinked. 'Yes. I'm okeh. I just — maybe it's the altitude, or the loop.' She managed a faint smile. 'Same thing happened to me this morning. I'm okeh, Claire. Is that enough? I think we should head back to the airfield.'

'Not yet,' Claire Delacroix shouted. 'Do we have enough fuel for a while longer?' She checked the fuel gauge on her own instrument panel. It read a quarter tank.

'Sure, enough for a while. What do you want me to do?'

'Follow the course you flew this morning, only lower. Can you fly at 1,000 feet or so?'

'Of course.'

Eleanor turned away from Claire. The SM-9 dropped toward the surface of San Francisco Bay. At this altitude the world looked very different from the cloud-dominated, rarified realm two miles above. Ships were visible moving in and out of the Golden Gate. The Marin headlands could be seen in the distance, and the East Bay hills as well. A few white specks on the surface of the Bay must be pleasure craft. Even in the hardest of times there were always the amateur sailors who could afford a boat and who had the time and love to take to the water on a clear day.

Claire Delacroix studied the compass on her control panel. The SM-9 was headed on a northerly course. She looked over the side of the monoplane. There, rising from the glinting waters of the Bay like a prehistoric leviathan awakened from the slumber of eons, she could see the fortified Alcatraz Island. It had been an army base since the 1850s. It had been used as a military prison during the war with Spain, and with the rise of gangs in the 1920's there was talk of turning it into a federal penitentiary, but for now it was still a fort.

As if she had read Claire Delacroix's mind, Eleanor Lown circled over the island. There was a large courtyard and Claire Delacroix could see a squad of soldiers at work there. It was not possible, from this altitude, to know for certain what they were doing, but Claire felt cold fingers clutch at her belly when she thought of what they might be cleaning up.

She didn't know Karol Raynor, had never met the Jugoslavian aviatrix, but Raynor was no less a human being for that, no less a fellow woman making her way in what was still a man's world. The thought of her plunging two miles from the aeroplane to smash against the waters of the Bay was something that Claire Delacroix could barely cope with, but the image of her after falling two miles, smashing into this ancient concrete courtyard was too horrid to contemplate.

The second SM-9, the aeroplane piloted by Andrew Sapphire, was now visible, flying at a higher altitude than Eleanor Lown and Claire Delacroix's ship. Sapphire was making maximum speed. Without discussion, Eleanor Lown gave chase to the other ship. How much of the by-play of moments ago Eleanor had seen, how much she understood, Claire Delacroix did not know. But clearly, Eleanor Lown's mind was now clear and she was pursuing Sapphire.

Two identical craft, each piloted by an expert aviator, one by a combat flier who had earned his rating as an ace in the Great War, the other by a gifted test pilot, raced through thin air above the waters and islands of San Francisco Bay. Soldiers drilling or working in the yard at Alcatraz, crewmen on merchant steamers at anchor in the Bay and frolickers enjoying the breeze and the sunlight aboard sailing craft, all marveled at the desperate contest taking place above their heads. Little did they realize its true and desperate meaning.

Sapphire curved in a westerly direction.

Eleanor Lown and Claire Delacroix followed suit.

Sapphire flew at a higher altitude. The atmosphere here was thinner than below and the SM-9's Wright radial gulped air furiously. Eleanor Lown climbed, racing to gain ground on Sapphire's ship. At this point, in this kind of contest between identical ships, every ounce of weight made a difference in the crafts' attainable speed. Ever so slowly, Andrew Sapphire drew away.

After a time, with Sapphire's aeroplane only a reddish glint in the sky ahead of her, Eleanor Lown swung her own craft around and headed back toward the Golden Gate. She shouted over her shoulder, 'Check the fuel gauge, Claire. We've reached the point of no return.'

Claire Delacroix pressed the heels of her hands against her forehead. Behind her protective goggles she closed her eyes and trusted to Eleanor Lown to guide them safely to their destination. In a few moments she dropped her hands and watched gratefully as the SM-9 passed above San Francisco Bay, dropping low over the water, racing its own dark shadow across the now-choppy surface. Then they were over the Island of Alameda and the tarmac at Sapphire-MacNeese.

Claire raised her eyes to the flagpoles atop the Sapphire-MacNeese hangar, reading the message of the fluttering flags and windsock.

Skillfully Eleanor Lown brought the sleek aeroplane in for a landing. The ship's wheels touched the tarmac, bounced once, then slowed as Eleanor reversed the pitch of the propeller, using the power of the Wright engine as a brake.

The Cierva gyroplane had preceded them and could be seen inside the hangar, being gassed up and serviced for her next flight, presumably back to her home in Oakland.

In minutes they were inside Carter MacNeese's office, drinking MacNeese's prewar *schnapps*. Leicester Jenkins had joined the assemblage and stood silent and stolid against one wall, observing the others. Abel Chase appeared much the worse for wear. Miraculously, he had apparently avoided serious injury in his plunge from the MS-9 and his sudden impact on the wing of the Cierva gyroplane but his clothing was ripped, his face and hands covered with grime and oil. An angry bruise was already appearing on his cheek and would surely darken and spread.

Eleanor Lown's hands shook as she lifted her mug to her lips. She swallowed a healthy slug of *schnapps*, coughed once and lowered her cup. 'I feel so guilty, Mac.'

'You were blameless, Eleanor.'

There were no more *misters* or *misses* or *doctors*. The events of the day had swept away all such formality, all such stiffness. They were men and women who had seen death up close and who had come within a hair's breadth of losing their own lives, all except for Carter MacNeese, and MacNeese's staying on the ground while the others were aloft e his emotional pain all the more agonizing.

'You were blameless,' he repeated. 'If only I had known, if any of us had known what Andrew was up to, we could have prevented this. I could have prevented it. Karol Raynor would be alive, and Andrew as well, of course.'

'I should have known,' Abel Chase put in. 'The pieces were all there, and I failed to put them together properly. The clue lay in our hospital ward in Staffordshire, Mac. When Aaron Saperstein charmed us all with his musicianship and his card tricks and his hypnotism. I just never thought of it as more than amusement. I never imagined that he would use his power to commit murder.'

The savant turned toward Eleanor Lown. 'It is obvious, now that the damage is done. When Andrew Sapphire took you and Karol Raynor aside before your flight this morning, he hypnotized you both. He instructed you, Eleanor, to hold your aeroplane upside down at the top of your loop-the-loop. He instructed Karol Raynor to wait for that moment, to anticipate the instant when she felt gravity tugging her out of her seat. He told her that she would be perfectly safe, that there was no need to hold on. And then he instructed both of you to forget that you had been hypnotized, to forget — consciously — that he had given you instructions, but to remember those instructions subconsciously and to carry them out when the moment came.'

Eleanor Lown began to weep, softly and steadily, tears rolling down her cheeks and soaking into her costume. Claire Delacroix put her arms around the other woman and patted her shoulders and back, knowing there was no way to assuage her grief but offering what small comfort she could.

'I didn't realize the passion that Saperstein felt toward the European monarchies. I suppose his people have suffered. He said that he hated war and he hated the dictators and kings of Europe. Remember how he carried on in the hospital, Mac? And today he was as impassioned as ever. Perhaps more so.'

'He couldn't see selling our ships to any of those powers.' MacNeese poured himself another generous jolt of *schnapps*. He drank half a cupful and wiped his mouth with his cuff. 'We debated it here in the office, Abel, hours on end. What you saw today was just a sample. I couldn't make him see that the Serbian royalists were any different from the Nazis or the Bolshevists. They were all the same to Andrew. To Aaron.' He gave the last words double meaning, raising his coffee mug in toast to his absent partner.

There was a long pause in the room, broken by the sound of another aeroplane coming in for a landing at another facility. From the sound of it, it was a twin-engined passenger liner, probably one of the brand-new, all-metal Boeing 247's.

'Do you think he has a chance?' Eleanor Lown had managed to regain control of herself and raise her tear-streaked face toward the others. 'Is there anywhere he can land?'

For the first time Leicester Jenkins spoke. 'Not a chance. From what you've said, he was too far out to sea to make it back. Those aeroplanes have no life rafts, have they? No life jackets or floats. And no parachutes, of course.'

Carter MacNeese said, 'No, Leicester. The pilots in the Great War considered it cowardly to wear a parachute. Old customs die hard.' He paused, then said, 'Our ships are built for speed and will be equipped for combat.'

Jenkins shrugged.

MacNeese struggled painfully to his feet and limped to the center of the room. 'You accomplished what I asked of you, Abel. I thank you.' There was grief as he extended his hand to Abel Chase.

The detective took the proffered hand in his own. 'I wish the answer to your puzzle had been less tragic, Mac. But it was good to renew our acquaintanceship face-to-face. I hope you will visit Claire and myself at the old homestead now.'

'I shall,' said MacNeese. 'And please send me a bill for professional services, Abel.'

'No need for that,' Chase murmured as he and Claire Delacroix headed for the exit, for the Hispano-Suiza, and for home.

Leicester Jenkins turned to Eleanor Lown. 'Ever been up in a gyroplane, Miss Lown? I'll wager you'll enjoy it. And you need something to take your mind off all that's happened today.'

Eleanor Lown managed a small, tentative smile for the massive Jenkins. She nodded her acceptance of the invitation.

A day later, or perhaps it was two or three, Abel Chase and Claire Delacroix sat watching the sunset from their places in the great Tudor manse high in the Berkeley hills. Claire Delacroix had attired herself once more in *kimono* and *obi*. Her hair was elaborately piled upon her head in the Japanese style, held in place with precious implements carved of purest jade. The soothing tones of her *shakuhachi* faded to silence. She reached for a jug of hot *saki* and poured a tiny cup for herself and another for Abel Chase, suppressing her impulse to ask if he had undergone an encounter with the legendary Manassa Mauler. His costume, of course, was impeccable and the grime and oil had been scrubbed from his

118

epidermis, but only time would remove the evidence of his scrapes and bruises.

Abel Chase and Claire Delacroix raised their *saki* cups. '*Banzai!*' sounded Chase's rich voice.

'*Banzai!*' echoed Claire Delacroix.

Abel Chase lifted a copy of that morning's San Francisco *Call*. 'Have you perused today's newspaper?' he asked his companion.

Claire Delacroix shook her head. 'No,' she said softly.

'I will read a dispatch,' Chase said. 'The header is, *Double Mystery — Are the Martians Here?* There is a byline, Burt van Hopkins.'

'I've read his stories in the *Call*,' Claire Delacroix responded. 'He's a good, responsible reporter. One of the best on the *Call*. I'm surprised to hear that van Hopkins is writing about Martians. What does the story say?'

Chase read: '*Coast Guard Commander Marion Tinsley informs the* Call *that the cutter under his command, USS Scorpio, picked up wreckage at sea near the Farallon Islands west of the Golden Gate.*

Zeron Horton, keeper of the lighthouse that has warned shipping away from the rocky Farallons since its construction in 1855, was quoted as saying, 'I heard a buzzing noise and then I swear, I saw this spaceship come crashing down. It was all shiny, red and white. There must have been Martians on it or somebody. They tried to land right on the island but you know it's just a pile of jagged rocks. The spaceship smacked right into the rocks and tumbled back into the water.

'Commander Tinsley has requested that anyone aware of a missing aircraft contact the Coast Guard immediately. He reports no evidence of survivors, but Lightkeeper Horton insists that at least one Martian was seen crawling on the rocks after the 'spaceship' crashed

'Earlier in the day, soldiers in the army garrison on Alcatraz Island stated that someone came crashing down from the sky. 'He or she or it landed on our drill field, narrowly missing a squad of artillerymen,' according to Major Francisco Mayer. 'Whoever or whatever it was,' Mayer added, 'we just scraped up *the remains and called the coroner's office. They sent out a boat and took it away.' Asked if he thought the decedent might be a Martian, Major Mayer declined comment.'*

Claire Delacroix shook her head ruefully. 'That wasn't a spaceship out at the Farallons, Abel. And that wasn't a Martian who fell onto Alcatraz.' Claire Delacroix raised her *saki* cup and peered across its rim, toward the Golden Gate and the far-distant Farallons, invisible in a thickening bank of fog.

'No, Delacroix,' Chase agreed, 'it was not a spaceship. Nor a Martian.'

3

The Case of the Dark Star

The high-ceilinged room was filled with the passionate notes of Dmitri Shostakovich's *Ledi Makbet Misenskogo Uyezda* pouring from the brilliantly-bowed 'cello of Claire Delacroix. The cellist read from a handwritten instrumental transcription of the aria, '*Shto znachit starost*'.'

A few paces away, Akhenaton Beelzebub Chase leaned over his ornately carved teakwood desk, a silver filigreed Waterman pen in hand. In perfectly trained Spencerian script he composed a personal letter.

My Dear Mr. DiMaggio:

I trust you will forgive a stranger for addressing you without formal introduction; I write to you in the capacity of an humble baseball fan who had the pleasure of seeing you perform in your three games with the San Francisco Seals during this past season of 1932.

There is no question in my mind that you are capable of playing at the highest level, despite your poor batting average of .222. I will append to this missive a few simple hints for the improvement of your hitting technique, which I can assure you, beyond the remotest doubt, will result in raising your batting average by a minimum of one hundred points. In addition, if I may make a further suggestion, I believe that your defensive talents would be more appropriately utilized as an outfielder, preferably a center-fielder, than they were this past year in the role of second baseman.

In regard to your approach to batting, it should have been obvious to any keen observer that —

At this point the sound of cast iron striking cast iron boomed through the house. As if rehearsed, Abel Chase laid his pen aside and Claire Delacroix lowered her bow. As the last note of the 'cello faded to silence Leicester Jenkins, Abel Chase's man of all work, crossed the room.

The heavy door swung open to reveal a uniformed figure silhouetted against the bright April sky above San Francisco Bay. From his position behind his desk, Abel Chase looked up, then smiled, circled the desk and advanced halfway to the door. Leicester Jenkins, livery-clad, stood aside as a muscular, uniformed individual strode rapidly, despite a slight limp, toward Abel Chase, his hand outstretched.

'Major Chase,' the blue-clad newcomer exclaimed.

'Captain Baxter,' Chase replied.

Cleland Baxter, captain of the San Francisco Police Department's homicide bureau, grinned as the two clasped hands. 'It's Captain Baxter to everyone else, Major, but I'll always be Corporal Baxter to you, sir.'

Chase put his arm around Baxter's blue-clad shoulders and led him across the room. 'You know Miss Delacroix, Cleland.'

Baxter nodded.

Claire Delacroix had risen from her seat and carefully laid aside her 'cello and bow. She extended a graceful hand to Captain Baxter, who blushed as if uncertain whether to bow over the extended hand and confer a kiss upon it, or simply to shake it. He settled upon the latter course. Claire Delacroix grinned.

Responding to an almost inaudible command from Abel Chase, Leicester Jenkins had left the room. After a brief absence he returned with a tray bearing a dark green bottle and two brandy snifters. In addition there was also a silver coffee service and a fine Spode cup and saucer. Cleland Baxter was settled now on a tapestry-covered sofa. Abel Chase and Claire Delacroix sat in matching wing-chairs, forming a conversational triangle with the police officer. Jenkins silently placed the tray on a low table between the sofa and chairs.

Abel Chase said, 'I won't embarrass you by offering alcohol while you're here on an official errand, Cleland. But I'll admit I'm surprised to receive you in broad daylight without advance warning or communication. And in uniform on a Sunday. You don't normally attend divine worship in uniform, do you? This is most unusual for you, if I may say so.'

While Jenkins silently prepared beverages for the three, Baxter leaned forward earnestly. 'No, it isn't that. The missus and I and the little ones got home from church and I was about to take the sprouts for a romp on the lawn while the missus fixed Sunday dinner when the telephone sounded. It was the Mayor in person. I'm here by direct order of hizzonor. He told me to put on my blues and head straight for the ferry slip and come to your house quick-time. My LaSalle is standing in your driveway this very minute, Major.'

Abel Chase nodded. 'The Mayor himself. Well, well. And how is Mr. Rossi these days?'

Baxter grimaced. 'He's digging in deeper every day, Major Chase. He's not so bad for an Italian, but I do miss Mayor Rolph, now that he's moved up to the mansion in Sacramento.'

Baxter lifted the green bottle from the service tray and added to his coffee. 'You do serve the finest coffee in town, Major, no doubt about it.'

Chase smiled. 'What was so urgent?'

'Mayor Rossi told me that he'd had a phone call from Mr. William Randolph Hearst himself. Mr. Hearst is down at San Simeon. He's having one of his fancy wingdings this weekend and one of the guests failed to show up.'

Abel Chase exchanged glances with Claire Delacroix. She sat warming a brandy snifter between her palms. 'Too bad about Mr. Hearst. I hope his party won't be ruined,' Abel Chase addressed Baxter. 'However, I don't see that this is of concern to the San Francisco Police Department. Surely not to the homicide bureau. And, Cleland, I might add that I am puzzled as to why the mayor sent you across the bay to visit me.'

Baxter looked around, a worried expression on his face.

'You may speak freely,' Abel Chase reassured him. 'Miss Delacroix is my confidante and assistant. Anything you tell me is safe with her. As for Jenkins, he is the exemplar of discretion.'

'You know the caliber of guests who attend Mr. Hearst's soirees,' Baxter said softly. 'The cream of the film colony. Mr. Fairbanks, Miss Pickford, Charlie Chaplin, young Gable, that Swede Garbo.'

'Indeed, Cleland. Miss Delacroix and I have participated in an occasional tennis match at San Simeon. I had a very pleasant chat with Colonel Lindbergh over whiskies before the fire at San Simeon one evening. As I recall, you absented yourself, Miss Delacroix.'

'Mr. Cooper invited me for a drive in his Duesenberg, Dr. Chase.'

Captain Baxter sat up straighter. 'Jackie Cooper?'

'No,' Claire Delacroix explained, 'Gary Cooper. It was a lovely night with a full moon overhead.'

'It sounds romantic.'

'It was all very proper, Captain. We even had a chaperone. Louella Parsons rode with us. I thought she'd never stop talking. Of course, Hollywood gossip is fascinating. I was amazed at some of the things I learned — if Miss Parsons is to be believed, of course.'

Abel Chase lowered his brandy snifter with a click that drew the conversation back to business. 'You were saying, Cleland — ?'

'Yes, sir. Well, Mr. Hearst's been very concerned about publicity ever since he shot Thomas Ince aboard his yacht.'

'Not surprising.' A mild note of irony sounded in Abel Chase's voice. 'Although I fail to understand the moral outrage of a married man whose mistress exchanges intimacies with a third party. Or should I say, a fourth. Besides, Hearst was aiming at Chaplin. The unfortunate Ince was the victim of poor marksmanship, not an unwise selection of paramours. Please, Cleland, do get to the point.'

'Yes, sir, I'm sorry.'

'Suppose you tell me just who has gone missing, Cleland, and under which circumstances he did so.'

'Surely, Major. I wonder if I might . . . ' Baxter indicated the silver service tray, and in response to Abel Chase's nod he proceeded to refill his cup. Before resuming speech he downed half its contents. 'First of all, it isn't any *he* that's missing. It's Miss del Sueño.'

A soft gasp escaped Claire Delacroix. 'Isabella del Sueño has gone missing?'

Baxter turned to face her. 'Yes, Miss. She was invited to Cambria for the weekend. According to Mayor Rossi, she phoned the Castle on Friday. She was working on her new film, *Scandal in Buenos Aires*. She was going to head for Cambria as soon as she got off work. They were filming on location up in the wine country near Napa.'

'Yes,' Chase put in. 'So I had heard. Please, Cleland.'

The uniformed police commander cleared his throat. 'Mayor Rossi says she'd ordered a new Pierce Arrow just before they started filming. She took the Coast Line from Los Angeles to San Francisco, picked up her car at Golden Gate Pierce on Van Ness, and drove on to Napa. Mr. Hearst's party started two days ago, on Friday. Miss del Sueño was supposed to be there. She phoned Cambria twice, just as she was leaving the studio and again from

Carmel-by-the-Sea.'

'What was she doing in Carmel?' Abel Chase asked.

'Nothing.' Baxter shook his head. 'Seems that the first time she called, she said she'd had a longer day on location than she expected, but she didn't want to miss Mr. Hearst's party so she was going to drive straight from Napa to the Castle in Cambria. Second time she called from Carmel. She said that the traffic had been heavier than she expected and she too tired to go on so she was going to spend the night in Carmel and drive on in the morning.'

'At what hour did Miss del Sueño place that call?'

'Oh, my, I'm not sure that Mayor Rossi mentioned that.' The police captain scratched his gray thatch of hair. 'Well,' he frowned with concentration, 'now that I work on it a little, I think he said something about it after all. I think it was four-thirty in the afternoon. But I don't see why that would matter.'

'Perhaps it matters, perhaps not. Please go on, Baxter.'

Captain Baxter lowered his cup and saucer to the table before him. 'That was the last anyone at the Castle heard from Miss del Sueño. Mr. Hearst and Miss Davies and the rest were waiting for her all yesterday. It was her birthday, don't you know. A mere nineteen years of age and already the most beautiful woman on the face of the Earth, if you believe the fan magazines. I've seen a couple of her talking pictures and I can believe it.' He raised his head and smiled sheepishly at Claire Delacroix. 'Present company excepted, of course. And the missus excepted, too, if she could hear me.'

Abel Chase rose from his wing chair. Hands clasped behind his back, he paced the flagstone floor of the great room, from the Fourteenth Century tapestry that hung on the north wall to the display of antique weaponry on the south. A large glass-fronted clock, its hands and face decorated with gold fancywork, stood beside the display. It sounded the hour softly. Chase withdrew a heavy pocket-watch from his silk waistcoat and checked it against the tall clock. He faced the others.

'If Mr. Hearst is so concerned over Miss del Sueño's disappearance, I should think he would call in the Carmel police. Or the Cambria force.'

Baxter made a grumbling sound deep in his throat. 'With respect, sir, the Carmel boys are a nice enough bunch, I know the chief down there, but you know all of them swamis and mystics and poets what make Carmel their campgrounds. The local force wouldn't know how to deal with a case like this one. And as for Cambria, why, they're hayseeds, if you don't mind my saying so.' He nodded vigorously in agreement with himself, then resumed.

'No, sir. Mr. Hearst went straight to the top, to the Mayor of San Francisco. The Mayor called on me because he knows we're friends, you and I. After all, you saved my life in the Great War, Major.'

'And you mine, Cleland,' Abel Chase interjected.

'Yes, sir. The way I see it, if word gets out there'll be headlines from coast to coast. Mr. Hearst don't want that. You

133

know what he said one time, the Mayor quoted it to me and I won't forget it. Mr. Hearst said, 'News is what somebody doesn't want printed, all the rest is advertising.' That was Mr. Hearst, all right. And he and the Mayor is thick as thieves, if you'll pardon my way of puttin' it, and Mr. Hearst wants this cleared up quickly and quietly. You're the man for the job, Major Chase.'

Abel Chase halted, standing stiffly behind Claire Delacroix's wing chair. 'What do you think, Miss Delacroix? Does the case sound worthy of our efforts? Do we really care enough about a missing star of the silver screen? I will confess ignorance of this Miss del Sueño. I would infer from her name that she is of the Latin persuasion.'

'I know something about her,' Claire Delacroix said. Her voice was low in pitch and volume, but it had a quality that carried it to the listener with persuasive force. Her platinum hair remained swept behind her well-formed head as she had arranged it so as not to distract from her attention to the musical score and the

134

demands of her instrument.

Abel Chase circled her chair and resumed his seat. He knew she was possessed of a photographic memory; many times her encyclopedic knowledge had proved helpful to him in solving cases that would have baffled the most accomplished of police detectives.

'Isabella Alejandra Orquidia Paloma del Sueño y Montalvo, born in Seville on March 17, 1908, the daughter of a family of ancient Bourbon nobility. Educated by private tutors, of course. Discovered by the famous producer James Watkins while vacationing in Monte Carlo.'

'Whoa! Hold on there.' An expression of puzzlement crossed Captain Baxter's features. 'Did you say Miss del Sueño was born in 1908?'

Claire Delacroix nodded her affirmation, as graceful a motion as that of a prima ballerina.

'But — now just a minute.' Baxter opened the top button of his uniform tunic and withdrew an automatic pencil and pocket notebook. As he scribbled in the notebook a deep furrow appeared between his heavy eyebrows. When he spoke again he seemed uncomfortable. 'If she was born in 1908, why, she'd be celebratin' her twenty-fifth birthday this year, and we know she's barely nineteen.'

'Ah, no, Captain Baxter.' Claire Delacroix's smile contained no trace of condescension. 'The studio chooses to make her nineteen. Nature and nativity make her twenty-five.'

A red-tailed hawk swept past the tall window and Claire Delacroix raised her eyes to follow its path. She drew her breath sharply at the raptor's beauty, then spoke once more.

'I suppose you learned that from Miss Parsons,' Abel Chase interjected. His tone did not indicate untinctured pleasure.

'That's right,' Claire Delacroix confirmed. 'So many screen personalities are the product of studio publicity departments. And why not? They make over their stars from hair-do to pedicure, they give them new names, why not provide biographies suitable to the world of glamour they would like everyone outside of Hollywood to believe they inhabit?

Those are the life stories we read in the glossy fan magazines.'

'Those of us who choose to read the fan magazines,' Abel Chase added acerbically. 'I think we need only ask a few more questions of Captain Baxter. Then he may be excused to return to his family while we set out to unravel this little mystery, Miss Delacroix.' He leaned forward and tapped a carefully manicured fingernail on Cleland Baxter's uniform-trousered knee.

'You say that Miss del Sueño phoned San Simeon from Carmel.'

'Yes, sir.'

'That's only a couple of hours from Cambria, even at night. A little bit odd that she didn't drive on, but if she was exhausted from her labors in Napa and her drive that far, something like 300 miles, I suppose she might have preferred to arrive refreshed Saturday morning rather than tired on Friday night.'

Chase rose again and resumed his pacing.

'Did she give the name of her hotel?'

'I think not,' Baxter stated. 'Of course,

everything I've got came through Mayor Rossi and my own boss, the Chief of Police.'

'Yes.' Chase pursed his lips, his carefully-maintained pencil moustache forming a horizontal line beneath his thin nose. 'It would have been better to get the information directly from Bill Hearst.'

'I thought of that myself,' Baxter said. 'Mayor Rossi told me that Mr. Hearst wanted to devote himself to his guests. He don't want us to call him back until we find Miss del Sueño.'

'Typical,' Abel Chase snapped, 'typical of Hearst. Very well, we shall play this game by his rules. It will make the victory all the sweeter when I find Señorita Isabella Alejandra Orquidia Paloma del Sueño y Montalvo and deliver her to San Simeon, safe and sound.'

He swung around. 'You had best put your 'cello in its case, Miss Delacroix, and change to a travelling outfit. Comrade Shostakovich and Signor DiMaggio will keep, I'm certain. Jenkins will warm up the Hispano-Suiza. Captain Baxter, please inform the Chief and the Mayor that the case is in my hands and will be resolved in short order.'

Cleland Baxter rose to his feet and extended his hand to Abel Chase. 'I've no doubt, sir, that you'll handle this as you do all your cases. And I'll be heading to my home, then.'

'Give my regards to your wife and daughters,' Abel Chase told him.

In less than an hour Leicester Jenkins had brought the Hispano-Suiza to the front of the house. The automobile's fuel tank, oil reservoir and water level were topped off and Chase's and Delacroix's valises had been carefully stowed in the phaeton's spacious luggage compartment. Jenkins himself, clad now in dark chauffeur's uniform and cap, stood holding the great car's door open.

'Will you want me to drive, sir?'

Abel Chase shook his head. 'Miss Delacroix and I will head for Carmel. We should be there by evening. You will hold yourself in readiness, Jenkins. If needs be I'll telephone, or Miss Delacroix will, and give you your instructions.'

'Yes, sir.' Jenkins affected a military

salute and a faint suggestion of a Prussian bow. 'I'll have the motorcycle ready to go. I can proceed directly on the two-wheeler or head to Oakland and fly on in the gyroplane.'

Abel Chase waited while Jenkins helped Claire Delacroix into the Hispano-Suiza's passenger seat, then slid his own lithe form behind the steering wheel. He did not comment on the leather-covered portfolio his companion placed beside herself. He put the car in gear, engaging its monstrous 720 horsepower V12 engine. The car rolled smoothly from the driveway onto the winding road through the Berkeley hills, through the city of Oakland, and onto the highway that would lead to the farm country around Salinas and the artists' colony of seaside Carmel.

As the Hispano hummed softly to itself, Claire Delacroix switched on the custom radio with which the great car was fitted. A powerful station beamed incidental music from Tchaikovsky's *Snow Maiden* into the tonneau. Claire Delacroix let the lovely sounds carry her away briefly, then she lowered the volume to permit conversation.

'So Señorita del Sueño is our prey,' she began.

'I would not bother with a case like this save for Captain Baxter's having asked me to intervene.'

'You've worked with him before. Forgive me, Dr. Chase, but I don't understand the relationship. You're a man of learning and refinement.'

'Yes,' Abel Chase agreed. 'I have accepted degrees from leading universities in Europe and the United States and it is true that I have been consulted from time to time by leading scholars and researchers in numerous fields.'

'And Captain Baxter is, well, to call him a diamond in the rough might be less than kind,' Claire Delacroix contributed.

The hills of southern Alameda County rose on either side of the macadam. It had been a rainy winter in northern California and the countryside was a tapestry of greens in every shade. Cattle grazed in fields on one side of the highway while spring vegetables grew in orderly rows on the other.

'Cleland Baxter was a corporal in a unit under my command in France. A fine soldier, courageous yet disciplined. An occasion arose, I'll tell you about it in detail some other time, Miss Delacroix, when his life was at stake and I had the privilege of saving him. And not long after that, he returned the favor. So you see, there is a bond between us. When we were mustered out, Baxter obtained his job with the San Francisco force and I acceded to the request of the University to teach an occasional course, and he has brought me such cases as he thinks I might find amusing.'

Chase swung the powerful Hispano-Suiza around a lumbering farm vehicle, then pulled back to the right. The soothing strains of the Tchaikovsky composition had given way to an energetic A minor violin concerto by Alexander Glazunov. There was no conversation for a time, until Abel Chase, frowning, addressed his companion.

'I didn't realize that you were so interested in cinema, Miss Delacroix.'

Claire Delacroix balanced her leather-bound portfolio carefully on her knees and opened its polished brass lock. From the portfolio she extracted a half dozen brightly-covered periodicals and spread them on her lap. Their titles were *Silver Screen Stories, Motion Picture Cavalcade, Movie Idols* and the like. All of them featured painted images of the same glamorously-posed young woman on their covers. Her hair was glossy black, worn in the longer fashion that was returning to replace the boyish look of the prior decade. Her sparkling eyes were the color of onyx; her skin, a glowing, healthy olive. Her figure suggested a voluptuosity, again in deep contrast to the flat rectangularity of the 1920's. Claire Delacroix studied the images with a sense of familiarity, then neatly stacked the periodicals and carefully slid them back into the portfolio.

'I brought a few fan magazines with me, Dr. Chase. Isabella del Sueño is featured in them. I thought they might prove helpful in tracking her down.'

'Good work, Miss Delacroix. I shall examine them when we reach Carmel. I imagine there are also biographies of the young woman in those magazines.' His tone indicated a low opinion of fan publications.

'There are.'

'You have managed to surprise me, Claire, not for the first time,' Abel Chase commented. 'I had thought you devoted your free time to more serious pursuits. Surely your musical talents are deserving of nurture.'

'You make me blush, Abel.'

She referred to him under most circumstances as Dr. Chase, and he to her as Miss Delacroix, but on occasion they would lapse into more familiar forms of address.

'I did not mean to do so,' Chase said.

'I suppose you could call it a guilty pleasure. I do sneak off to a movie now and then.'

'You time is your own, of course, when you are not performing the duties for which you are paid.'

'And I like to read about the stars. Their world seems like a living fairy tale, at least as portrayed in the fan magazines.

The experience of Isabella del Sueño is like a fantasy. There was a version of her life story in *True Hollywood* magazine that held me fascinated. The author claimed to have visited Isabella at her cottage on location while they were shooting *Ride, Vaquero* and got the inside scoop. You know, Isabella's horse had shied at a rattlesnake and threw her. She was so brave, she wanted to go right back to work, but her co-star insisted that the director give her the rest of the day off. That was Roland Ramirez. The actor, I mean. The director was Eberhard Kasper.'

Abel Chase shook his head. 'You amaze me, Claire. A woman of your intelligence and talent filling her head with such trivialities.'

'Oh, I know it's all silliness. But forgive me this one foible, won't you, Abel?'

The only response was a grunt, which Claire Delacroix took as a sign of assent.

'The del Sueño family are descended from Castillian royalty dating back to the Twelfth Century. They're first cousins of the present King of Spain. Isabella's parents are the *Conde y Condesa de Sevilla*. Isabella has an older sister who volunteered as a nurse on the Italian front in the Great War. Of course Isabella was just a baby when the war began, so there was no way she could contribute to the cause. But don't you think it possible that her sister nursed you after you were wounded? You said that Captain Baxter saved your life, so I assume you were wounded, Abel, weren't you?'

'I was gassed. I suppose that qualifies as a wound. The Army thought so, at any rate, and awarded me a Purple Heart to go with my Silver Star. But that was in France. There wasn't much fighting in Italy, if any.'

'Anyway, Isabella's sister came home safely and they lived an idyllic life on their *estancia* near Seville while little Isabella grew up. Then when the lovely Maria Gonsalves Escobar died so tragically in that airplane crash — you do remember Maria Gonsalves Escobar, Abel, don't you, even though you look down on the movies?'

'I do,' he growled.

'Well, Maria's favorite producer, James Watkins, and the director, Eberhard Kasper — there was a rumor of a lurid triangle involving Maria Escobar and Kasper and Watkins, you know — both Watkins and Kasper were utterly prostrated by the loss. They went into seclusion together on the French Riviera, and Irene Morton, the actress, managed to get Herr Kasper to motor over to Monte Carlo while James Watkins stayed behind studying some scripts. And there on the beach Kasper was stunned by the beauty of this young Spanish girl who was vacationing with her family.'

'And she was none other than Isabella del Sueño, of course.' The irony in Chase's voice was cutting.

'Yes, she was! Her sister was there, acting as chaperone, but Herr Kasper took one look at Isabella and decided that she was the only woman in the world who could possibly replace Maria Gonsalves Escobar.'

'And that was the beginning of her career,' Abel Chase furnished.

'Yes.'

'And every word of it is true, is it not?'

There was a lengthy moment during which the melodic strains of the Glazunov composition were the only sounds to be heard in the tonneau of the Hispano-Suiza. Finally Claire Delacroix answered Abel Chase's question.

'I believed the *True Hollywood* story when I read it. I know you'll think I'm incredibly naïve, Abel, and I suppose I am. But when Gary Cooper took me for a ride in his Duesenberg he told me that he'd actually escorted Miss del Sueño on several occasions and the *True Hollywood* story was all made up by the studio publicity department. He said that the fan magazines are simply full of fairy tales.'

'And what did Miss Parsons say about that? You did say she went along for the ride, didn't you?'

'Louella said it was all true. I mean, what Gary Cooper told me about the magazines, not the things that they print in them.'

Abel Chase said, 'The human understanding is like a false mirror, which, receiving rays irregularly, distorts and discolors the nature of things by mingling its own nature with it.'

'In other words, you're saying that it's hard to know what is real.'

'Did I say that? Actually, it was Francis Bacon who said that. He was a wise man. My ideal as an inquirer after truth. Francis spoke also of lucid intervals and happy pauses. I commend his works to you.'

The Hispano-Suiza topped a gentle hill and before them spread the town of Carmel-by-the-Sea, and beyond it the sparkling water of a gentle, curving bay. The town itself was laid out after the fashion of an English village, with narrow thoroughfares and buildings in the old Tudor style.

Abel Chase guided the Hispano-Suiza to a place in the driveway of a hostelry that combined the charm of old England with elegance and the promise of modern convenience. A main building presented the appearance of a baronial hall while half-beamed stucco cottages ranged to left and right. The name of the establishment was featured in a discreet wooden sign beside the main entrance.

The Sussex Downs.

Chase turned over the keys to a concierge and obtained for himself and his companion the use of a pleasant cottage comprising two bed chambers and a sitting room. By the time Abel Chase and Claire Delacroix had settled their belongings in their respective quarters and made their way to the central lodge's cocktail lounge the sun was setting and the room was filled with a golden refulgence.

A notice had been posted on the announcement board just outside the lounge. Claire Delacroix blinked as she passed it, recording the message on the photographic emulsion of her mind. *Sri Mehadi Nurmada Kavinda Conducts Sunrise Service and Purification of the Soul Daily at Carmel Beach — All Are Welcome.*

Nearby a small library had been created for the convenience of hotel guests. Even at a distance Chase recognized the bindings of a number of reference works, some of them thoroughly mundane, others remarkable for their esoteric nature.

Over cocktails with Claire Delacroix, Chase outlined his strategy for finding the missing motion picture star. 'I trust you will be available to assist me and to make notes as I pursue this little puzzle, Miss Delacroix. We should have it cleared up and return to Berkeley in quick time. Classes resume shortly at the University and I do not wish to disappoint my students.'

The management had furnished a fine, single-malt Scotch whiskey for the pair, along with light snacks. Claire Delacroix sipped sparingly at her beverage, then asked her employer, 'What is our program?'

Abel Chase laughed. 'The case is so obvious and so simple, I would normally have turned it down, save as a favor to my friend Cleland Baxter.' He reviewed the facts: 'Miss del Sueño telephoned San Simeon from Carmel, stating that she was too fatigued to drive on to Cambria.'

He reached for the tray of tiny sandwiches that stood between himself and Claire Delacroix. He extended the tray to her and waited while she helped herself to a square of white bread topped with a bit of cheese and a sprig of watercress. He did the same, and when he had swallowed the morsel he followed it with a sip of whiskey.

Abel Chase had changed from his travelling outfit to a jacket of soft tweed, a four-in-hand tie of quiet pattern, and flannel trousers. Claire Delacroix wore a satin blouse of midnight blue, offsetting her platinum hair that now hung softly over her shoulders, and a floor-length skirt.

'All I need do is find the hostelry where Isabella del Sueño spent Friday night and pursue her track from that point,' Abel Chase explained.

'Yes, but how will you do that?'

'Carmel-by-the-Sea is not that large a community, and there are few hotels here. Surely a movie star of Miss del Sueño's magnitude, if she is indeed as major a figure as both Captain Baxter and you suggest, would have been noticed. Nor are there many new Pierce Arrows in these streets. In fact, I think I've seen more bare-footed swamis and turban-wearing pilgrims in Carmel than I've seen in all my life. Surely Isabella del Sueño would have made an indelible impression.'

'Fair enough,' Claire Delacroix conceded, 'but what if she doesn't turn up in Carmel? Surely you have prepared further options.'

'I will find Isabella del Sueño, of that you may rest assured, Claire.'

They proceeded to the dining room and shared a fresh seafood dinner derived from the local catch. There was an advantage, Abel Chase remarked, in living near a major fishing port. The meal was accompanied by fresh-baked bread and a fresh *gewürztraminer* imported from the wineries of the Napa Valley.

Following a dessert of strawberry tarts, coffee and brandy, Abel Chase borrowed one of Claire Delacroix's motion picture fan magazines and invited her to accompany him as he questioned the manager of the hotel. Claire Delacroix, however, pleading a slight feeling of stuffiness, asked instead to be permitted a solitary stroll out of doors.

The great sleuth accompanied his protégée to the exit of the hotel. Despite the hour shops were open and tourists chattered gaily as they made their way from one to another. Among the well-dressed and clearly well-to-do there was also an admixture of men in turbans and women in caftans, their eyes rimmed with kohl and their foreheads anointed with caste marks of dubious authenticity. Concluding that the village streets were safe for a lone woman, Abel Chase bid his assistant to venture from the hotel on her own.

Returning to the lobby, Chase sought the manager and requested a private interview.

The manager, one Dismas Grey, ushered Chase into his office. Grey sported an excess of wavy blonde hair and a moustache to match. He was clad in a well-cut suit of dark serge, a white broadcloth shirt and necktie of maroon silk. He averred that he had heard of Chase and was honored to have him as a guest in his establishment. What, he inquired, could he do to be of assistance?

Before giving any details, Chase secured Grey's promise of confidentiality. He then sketched for the *hotelier* the information provided him by Cleland Baxter. At the end of his presentation he laid the fan magazine he had borrowed from Claire Delacroix on Grey's desk.

As Grey reached for the magazine, Chase noted the manager's cufflinks of green jade carved in a peculiar pattern. Not three men in America would have recognized the carving, and Abel Chase was one of them. It was a Tibetan mandala, the Secret Sign of Lhasa.

'I recognize the young woman,' Grey said softly. 'It was a most unusual incident. She arrived late Friday afternoon, driving her own Pierce Arrow. She registered and paid in advance for her room. The name she used was not, however, del Sueño. If you wish, we can consult the hotel register, but in fact I remember quite vividly the lady's arrival and the name under which she registered.'

'Your word will suffice,' Chase nodded.

'Indeed. She did not use the pen which

is kept with the hotel register, but instead used one of her own, a truly fine Schaeffer. I am something of a fancier of fine writing instruments, you see.'

'What name did she use?'

'She wrote her name as Zetta Vidonia Oroso. I was at the desk myself when she registered, and I must confess that I was taken aback. Of course I was most impressed by her Pierce Arrow automobile, and she was a person of quite striking appearance, somewhat dark complexioned and with glossy, jet-black tresses. Between her features and her first name I suspected that she might be of . . . '

Dismas Grey paused and tented the fingers of both hands beneath his chin. He appeared to be waiting for a sign from Abel Chase that the sleuth had mentally completed the sentence. When Chase failed to offer any such sign, Grey continued.

' . . . the Hebrew persuasion.'

Still Chase remained silent. After a pause punctuated only by the sound of an automobile horn from the narrow street outside the hotel, Grey spoke again.

'Of course we try to remain broadminded in all matters at the Sussex Downs, but we do draw the line somewhere. One must, do you not agree?' This time he did not wait for a response but continued, holding the fan magazine Chase had shown him in one well-manicured hand and studying the portrait on the magazine's cover. 'We often welcome as guests those pilgrims and truth-seekers who regard our little village as a spiritual Mecca. Surely you noticed the announcement board outside our lounge. But still, we maintain a restricted policy when it comes to registered guests.'

Abel Chase fixed the manager with eyes that had stared down death at the bayonet point of the Kaiser's soldiers as well as the revolvers of murdering gangsters.

Dismas Grey looked away. He lowered the fan magazine to his desk and slid it toward Chase. 'But you see, Miss Oroso had already registered. We usually maintain a polite fiction of being overbooked when certain persons request lodging, but in this case it was too late. Even so, Miss

Oroso had no sooner procured a room and seen to the disposition of her luggage than she left the premises and has not returned since.'

Chase cleared his throat unnecessarily, then asked, 'For how many nights did Miss Oroso pay?'

'Three.'

'She still occupies her cottage, then, in theory?'

Grey smoothed his blonde moustache carefully with his finger. 'As the cottage is paid for, it is in theory hers, yes.'

'Her luggage is there?'

'Yes.'

'Where is her automobile?'

'In order to maintain the rustic atmosphere of accommodations for our guests, the hotel provides garage space for their automobiles. The grounds are thus free of such modern intrusions. The Pierce Arrow is still there.'

'All right,' Chase said. He pushed his chair away from Grey's desk and strode back and forth in his habitual manner, hands clasped behind his back, his eyes focused on the carpet beneath his polished shoes. The carpet was of an oriental weave of complex pattern such as might capture the attention and occupy the mind for long periods.

'May I infer that no missing persons report was filed with the local authorities?'

Grey removed the display handkerchief from his jacket and dabbed it upon his forehead before returning it carefully to its place in his breast pocket. 'I will be candid with you, sir. I was not altogether comfortable having Miss Oroso as a guest and I was just as pleased with her absence. Further, there had been no indication of foul play or other irregularity. I felt no obligation to speak with the local police, nor did I do so.'

He reached for the fan magazine, which still lay on his desk and pushed it pointedly to the edge of the desk nearest Abel Chase. 'And now, sir, if you will excuse me, I have many duties to perform.'

Both men rose to their feet. 'Would it be possible,' Chase asked, 'to see Miss Oroso's cottage?'

Frowning, Grey said, 'Absolutely not. The privacy of our guests is paramount with this establishment. And may I ask how long a stay you have planned, Mr. Chase?'

'I prefer the title of Doctor, Mr. Grey. Miss Delacroix and I will be staying at your establishment no longer than is necessary.'

It was by no means difficult for Chase to locate the cottage assigned to Miss Oroso, whose true identity he was certain was identical to that of Señorita del Sueño. By strolling casually though the grounds surrounding the Sussex Downs he noted signs of life in most of the cottages. From some could be heard the sounds of laughter. In others, lights might be seen and figures cast mobile silhouettes upon curtains. Only two or three cottages remained to be investigated, and the conspicuous return of their occupants from a late dinner or other activities removed one of these from consideration.

Chase returned to his own room and removed a small but powerful flashlight from his valise. He sent its beams through an opening in the curtains of one darkened cottage. There were no signs of habitation; perhaps the guest who had reserved the accommodation had been delayed, or perhaps the Sussex Downs was not in fact fully booked for this night.

That left a single darkened cottage to be investigated.

Using skills learned through years of study and practice. Abel Chase was able to enter the cottage silently and without being observed. His flashlight possessed a movable shutter after the fashion of an old-style dark-lantern. By keeping the shutter at a narrow setting Chase was able to send forth a beam of light that illuminated its target brightly but was virtually invisible to any but himself.

Yes, there upon a folding stand he observed a tastefully designed woman's valise. Before examining the valise Chase crossed the room to a large closet. He opened it and shone the flashlight within. The closet contained feminine garments of the highest quality and latest fashion. The piece of luggage sported a brass lock but a quick examination revealed that the lock was there for show or perhaps as a token of security, rather than as an obstacle to anyone with the skills and tools required to open it.

In a matter of seconds Chase worked the lock open and lifted the lid of the valise. The contents were unremarkable save for the smartness of their design and the quality of manufacture. Surely these were the belongings of a woman with elevated taste and a generous budget.

But there was nothing in either the valise or the closet to suggest the whereabouts of the missing star.

Beside the bed stood a night table of dark polished wood. The drawer slid open smoothly revealing a Bible of the type commonly furnished in hotel rooms and a slick-paper magazine. Intrigued, Chase picked up the magazine. It was the May issue of *The Atlantic Monthly*. An envelope had been inserted between the pages of the magazine so as to serve as an impromptu bookmark. Chase turned back the pages and saw that the previous reader had marked the opening page of *The Autobiography of Alice B. Toklas*, by Gertrude Stein.

Chase removed the envelope, dog-earing the page to preserve the reader's place. The envelope was addressed to a post office box in Los Angeles. It bore no return address, but the green two-cent stamp carried a cancellation mark of Monterey, California. The name of the addressee was unfamiliar to Abel Chase.

This indeed was strange. Chase had expected to find the name of the missing star on the envelope, whether rendered as Señorita Isabella del Sueño or as Miss Zetta Vidonia Oroso. But the name on the envelope was neither. How many names did this woman use, Chase wondered, and what was their purpose?

A pasteboard rectangle gave the envelope its stiffness. Chase turned back the flap, noting that it had been carefully opened with a sharp blade. He removed the pasteboard. It was an elaborately engraved invitation, that much was obvious. Its text was rendered in two scripts, with both of which Abel Chase was thoroughly familiar.

Slipping the invitation into his pocket,

Chase replaced the now empty envelope in *The Atlantic Monthly*, then returned the magazine to the night table drawer and slid the drawer shut. He had already closed the closet and now he lowered the lid of the valise and snapped the brass lock shut.

He let himself out of the cottage and walked rapidly back to the baronial lodge. He had left no sign of his intrusion in Miss Oroso's cottage. If the missing actress returned she would find nothing out of order unless she looked for the invitation that Chase had removed from *The Atlantic*. In that case, he surmised, she might be puzzled or even distressed, but she would have no reason to suspect that a burglar had been at her things during her absence.

In the lobby of the Sussex Downs a group of guests had apparently spilled over from the crowded lounge and stood or sat in clusters, consuming beverages and exchanging views of the world. Chase heard talk of events in Washington, London, Berlin and Moscow. The names of dictators flew about as if they were the equal of Babe Ruth, Gertrude Ederle, Jean Harlow or Rudolph Valentino.

Abel Chase peered into the library. He had thought to consult the reference books contained therein in his study of the invitation he had removed from Zetta Vidonia Oroso's cottage, but several other guests were using the library and he dared not risk showing the pasteboard rectangle in their presence.

He permitted himself to emit a small sigh of disappointment, but without further delay he left the main lodge and made his way to the cottage that he had engaged for himself and Claire Delacroix. The door to Miss Delacroix's bedroom was closed. Presumably she had returned from her sojourn and retired for the night. Chase frowned as he ascertained the hour, then he slipped his pocket watch back into its place and settled himself on a hard wooden chair at the writing desk in a corner of the room.

He placed the invitation in the center of the desk, then opened a drawer and extracted a sheet of Sussex Downs stationery. He took his fine Waterman from the inner pocket of his jacket, unscrewed its cap and set himself to work

The two scripts used on the invitation were dramatically different. One of them Chase immediately recognized as Hebrew. The other was the familiar Latin script, although a variety of diacritical marks were far less familiar than in Chase's prior experience.

The Hebrew letters caused him to pause momentarily and recall his parents, both long dead. They had been brilliant scholars, the greatest team of archaeologists in their profession. Chase's mother had been an Egyptologist; his father, a Mesopotamiologist. Each accompanied the other on expeditions, offering the perspective of the contrasting culture to the pyramids, Sphinx, cyclopean temples, ancient tombs and cryptic hieroglyphics of the Pharaohs, or the ziggurats, gryphons, and long-deserted cuneiform writing of forgotten Babylon.

The Chases had named their son for two figures from the ancient world, the great and tragic Pharaoh Akhenaton and the Babylonian deity Beelzebub. They had maintained homes in London, New York, and San Francisco, moving among them when not engaged in their scholarly researches. Their son possessed dual British and American citizenship.

It was upon such a trip, traveling in a first class cabin on the maiden voyage of the ill-starred *Titanic*, that the senior Chases faced seemingly certain death for the first time, the irony of this fact in cruel contrast to the risks they had willingly taken in the Middle East in the pursuit of knowledge.

Their son was a student at the time. His parents believed that he was resident at an exclusive preparatory school in the State of Vermont but in fact he had disappeared from the school's authorities and was engaged in explorations of his own in the pre-Incan ruins of northwestern Peru. It was this isolation that spared him from the first reports of the *Titanic's* disastrous encounter with an iceberg in the North Atlantic.

Chase's mother had been offered a place in one of the great ship's lifeboats but chose instead to remain with her husband. Early reports listed them among the 1,503 souls lost in the icy Atlantic on that dreadful day in April of 1912. By the time young Abel, as he was already known, returned to the relatively civilized confines of Cuzco, it was known that the senior Doctors Chase were among the fortunate survivors of the mid-ocean calamity.

Three years later, the two Doctors Chase were returning to the British Isles from a sojourn in the United States. They had booked passage on the steamship *Lusitania* and were among the 1,201 individuals reported missing after the Kaiser's *Unterseeboot Zwanzig*, under command of *Kapitan* Walther Schwieger, torpedoed the *Lusitania*.

By now Abel Chase was a precocious fifteen-year-old university freshman. And this time there was no later bulletin reversing the loss of his parents. United States Secretary of State William Jennings Brian protested to the Kaiser's emissaries in Washington and to the Foreign Ministry in Berlin, but no further action was taken.

Young Chase followed the diplomatic maneuvering in each day's press, but when President Wilson indicated that the United States would maintain a policy of watchful waiting rather than intervene in the European conflict he could delay no longer. He withdrew from matriculation, crossed the border into Canada, and volunteered for service. Many Americans were doing the same; lying about one's age was a common practice. It helped that young Chase was mature-looking for his age, and the Canadian recruiters were happy to have these volunteers and tended to be credulous about their claims regarding age.

By the time the United States finally entered the Great War, Akhenaton Beelzebub Chase was Captain Chase of the Canadian fusiliers. He transferred to the United States Army and by virtue of his experience in trench warfare and gas attacks he was soon Major Chase. It was in his capacity as a battalion commander in the famed Rainbow Division that he first encountered Corporal Cleland Baxter, later Captain Cleland Baxter of the San Francisco homicide squad.

Now, seated at the writing desk in a rented cottage in Carmel-by-the-Sea, he called upon the knowledge of ancient languages he had absorbed from earliest childhood.

The Hebrew lettering was easily transliterated; determining its meaning only slightly less so. The pasteboard document invited the addressee to a religious observance, the Hebrew practice of *bar mitzvah*, to take place in the fishing community of Monterey. The celebrant was identified as *Isaac Laudalino Fonseca*.

The invitation itself was printed in glossy black letters. It bore a pair of signatures, rendered carefully by hand, also in Hebrew characters: *Xuxa Martina Oroso Fonseca and Simao Timote Fonseca*.

There was something familiar about one of those names. Abel Chase closed his eyes in concentration. He ran his hand through his hair, striving to identify the source. Then at last he had it: the key name was *Oroso*. Dismas Grey, the

170

manager of the Sussex Downs, had recognized the fan magazine portrait of Isabella del Sueño but he had told Chase that the actress had signed the hotel register as Zetta Vidonia Oroso.

Isaac Laudalino Fonseca was the *bar mitzvah* celebrant and Zetta Vidonia Oroso, known to millions of movie fans as Isabella del Sueño, had received an invitation to his *bar mitzvah*. She had checked into the Sussex Downs, telephoned William Randolph Hearst at San Simeon to announce her delay in arriving at his weekend affair, and disappeared.

She must have proceeded to Monterey to attend Isaac Laudalino Fonseca's *bar mitzvah*.

Further thought was required. Dismas Grey had stated that Señorita del Sueño, using the name Zetta Vidonia Oroso, had left her Pierce Arrow automobile at Sussex Downs. Perhaps she had hired a car or taxicab in Carmel-by-the-Sea. That could be checked, of course. But if she was in some way connected to Isaac Laudalino Fonseca, as the invitation indicated that she was, then someone, some relative of Isaac Fonseca's or a family friend, might well have driven from Monterey to Carmel-by-the-Sea and furnished transportation for the actress.

Abel Chase consulted his pocket watch. The hour was late. His neck was sore from bending over the invitation and his head ached. He rose and exited the cottage. The sky was clear and a million stars sparkled overhead. A gentle breeze whispered through the pine trees that dotted the grounds of the Sussex Downs.

Chase returned to the cottage and held the pasteboard rectangle in one hand. The segment of the invitation printed in Latin characters was incomprehensible to him save for the names of Isaac Laudalino Fonseca, Xuxa Martinha Oroso Fonseca, and Simao Timote Fonseca. There was no doubt in Abel Chase's mind that the message was the same as that which he had painstakingly translated from Hebrew.

He entered the cottage and climbed into bed. As he stared at the ceiling he realized that he had failed to convert the date on the invitation from the Hebrew calendar to the Gregorian.

He let his mind wander to past days, happy days before the deaths of his parents. They had taken him on digs in both Mesopotamia and Egypt, taught him to read the scripts of both empires as well as those of the ancient Phoenicians, Hebrews, and Hellenes. As if a motion picture machine were projecting images on the ceiling, he saw himself as a boy, accompanying his parents as they entered a tomb undisturbed for millennia.

His father was a man of less than average height. Born to a poor family in London's East End, Bertram Chase had struggled for survival as a message runner, sometime stevedore and more than occasional thief of freight from the docks along the Thames. Undernourished as a child, he had never attained his potential stature, but he built both his muscles and his mind until he was that oddity, a cockney-speaking, all but muscle-bound intellectual.

Chase's mother was as different from his father as could be imagined. Born in Simla of Anglo-Indian parents, Bettina

Winifred St. Sulpice had been sent 'home' to England to be educated by private tutors while her own parents maintained the lifestyle and authority of the Raj. Innately aristocratic of mien, Bettina had grown to a breathtaking beauty, slim, raven-haired, striking of feature and fascinating of manner. On occasion she would take ship for India to visit her parents and renew her Asian roots.

The aristocrat and the longshoreman met when Bettina, returning from a visit to India, spied a muscular youth making off with a treasured hatbox belonging her. To the amazement of all concerned she pursued him along the East India Dock Road until she caught up with him and threw him to the ground. The astonished young man at first laughed at the foolhardiness of this slip of a girl, his amusement mixed with admiration at her courage.

Amusement turned to dismay as the young woman demonstrated the martial arts she had learned in Asia.

Rather than turn the young man over

to the police, she befriended him, becoming his mentor and his tutor as her own education proceeded. In turn they wed, to the alarm and shock of both their families. Bertie and Betty became the oddest couple of the archaeological world, but none denied their mutual affection or the brilliance with which both pursued their work.

Akhenaton Beelzebub Chase's childhood had been happiest when he was with his parents, exploring ancient ruins and studying long-dead cultures. His years at boarding school had been less so. His adult life had begun on that dreadful day in 1915 when he learned of the sinking of *Lusitania* and the death of both his parents.

He closed his eyes and drifted off to a sleep troubled by dreams of icebergs and German torpedoes, of sinking ships and drowning passengers.

★　★　★

Claire Delacroix needed no alarm clock to awaken her at the hour of her choice.

She had long since trained herself, upon retiring for the night, to set a timer within her own brain. She knew from long experience that when she did so she would awaken at the time she had selected.

While safely away from the Sussex Downs on Sunday evening and free of prying eyes and ears, she had done her investigating and placed her telephone call through the agency of a local exchange. She had walked to the beach where the following morning's sunrise service was to be held, then returned to the Sussex Downs and retired.

Now, in the early hours of Monday morning, while the sky was still dark, she rose, showered and dressed. Her clothing was informal. It was heavy enough to keep her comfortable in the pre-dawn chill that she knew she would encounter.

As she left the cottage she noticed the pasteboard square that Abel Chase had worked on the previous night. In the darkened room it stood out like a ghostly presence. There was no sign of Chase himself. Claire Delacroix studied the pasteboard, unable to read either its Hebrew text or the accompanying rendition in Latin letters.

Next she picked up Chase's painstakingly rendered translation of the Hebrew words. A low, almost inaudible gasp escaped her. Instantly she memorized the names on the invitation.

Silently she left the cottage and retraced her footsteps of the previous evening. By the time she reached the beach a crowd of spiritual seekers had assembled there. They stood in perfect silence. Some wore ordinary street clothes; others, robes of white or maroon or saffron; some were barefoot, some wearing sandals; some bareheaded, others with cloth headdresses of varied design.

Claire turned to observe the way she had come. The road leading from the beach ran toward the low buildings of Carmel-by-the-Sea and onward, guiding the eye to the gently rounded hills beyond. As she watched, the first rays of the sun appeared in the sky.

Now Claire turned once more, back toward the beach. A moment ago there had been no sign of Mehadi Nurmada Kavinda, but now the spiritual leader stood facing her congregation. She wore a simple gown of what appeared to be white linen. As Claire watched, the sun's rays illuminated her hair, then her face, then her white-clad body. She raised her arms in benediction. A murmur rippled through the crowd.

Mehadi Nurmada Kavinda began to preach, a seamless amalgam of half a dozen Eastern and Western philosophies. To Claire Delacroix it was a familiar brew but Mehadi Nurmada Kavinda's followers were rapt.

There was a touch on Claire Delacroix's elbow. She turned and looked up to see the face of Leicester Jenkins. He was clad in a leather jacket, tight trousers and a motorcyclist's boots. He wore a soft leather helmet like that of an aviator, the goggles pushed onto his forehead and the chin straps hanging loose.

He gestured silently with his head. Claire followed the direction of the gesture with her eyes. Jenkins' Indian motorcycle stood against a tree some hundred yards up the street.

Together the two of them walked to the two-wheeler. When they reached the motorcycle Jenkins said, 'I've brought you a helmet and jacket, Miss.' The Indian's four-cylinder Ace engine gave off heat in the morning chill.

Claire Delacroix waited while Jenkins opened a saddlebag strapped to the Indian motorcycle. He handed her the leather garments and she slipped her arms into the sleeves of the jacket, then pulled the helmet over her platinum hair. She asked if the motorcycle was fully fuelled and Jenkins assured her that it was.

'All right,' she said. 'I have to place a telephone call before we go.' She checked her wristwatch, nodded in satisfaction, and returned to the telephone exchange. She obtained a number from Central and asked the operator to make her connection.

Shortly she rejoined Leicester Jenkins and spoke a few words. The man-of-all-trades nodded and settled onto the motorcycle. He was a big man, both taller and heavier than Abel Chase. Claire Delacroix climbed onto the seat behind him. Jenkins kicked the machine into life, looked around for early morning automobile traffic, and pulled into the street.

Jenkins steered the Indian motorcycle through the thoroughfares of Carmel-by-the-Sea and onto the shore road that would lead to Monterey. By the time they reached that town of fishing fleets and canneries the day was well established. An onshore breeze brought the scent of the Pacific Ocean and Monterey Bay to them. There was the sound of barking sea lions.

The motorcycle roared onto Wave Street. Claire Delacroix leaned forward and shouted instructions to Jenkins. He maneuvered the motorcycle through hilly thoroughfares. Behind them the sun sparkled on the bay. Black dots of otters and sea lions popped to the surface, then disappeared once again. The shapes of fishing vessels stood against the shining surface of the bay.

Soon the motorcycle drew to the edge of the street. Jenkins turned and asked

180

Claire Delacroix if this was the destination she had in mind. She told him it was and asked him to wait while she made her way to the building.

Behind a tidy lawn the small synagogue was hardly distinguishable from neighboring structures. Only stained glass windows featuring a Star of David and the Tablets of the Law identified the building to passersby. The doors were unlocked.

Claire Delacroix entered the synagogue quietly. Once inside she could hear the chanting which had been inaudible from the street.

She found herself standing in the rear of a sanctuary that held some fifty or sixty individuals. A railing separated rows of pews. Those on one side were filled by women; those on the other, by men.

At the front of the room a massive, elderly man wearing a black robe and white prayer shawl with blue markings stood facing a boy. The boy wore an obviously new blue suit, white shirt, black tie and skull cap. Like the older man, he wore a prayer shawl. Each of them held a small book. They were chanting, alternately, in a language Claire Delacroix could only guess was Hebrew.

Claire Delacroix had no idea how long the ceremony had been in progress or how soon it would end. She made her way to the women's section of the synagogue and found a place beside a woman whom she recognized despite her inconspicuous costume and lack of facial makeup.

The woman shot a querulous glance at the newcomer. Claire murmured a soft phrase. The woman replied shortly and gestured. Claire nodded.

Not until the service ended did the woman turn and speak to Claire, her voice pitched to prevent others from overhearing. She demanded to know how Claire knew who she was and why she would be in Monterey.

Even as the woman spoke she was guiding Claire by the elbow toward the back of the room. The rest of the persons present had moved in the opposite direction, clustering around the boy and the bearded man, offering loud congratulations to the boy and to the middle-aged couple, obviously his parents, who stood proudly behind him.

'This is the first time I've seen a *bar mitzvah*,' Claire confessed. 'In fact, it's the first time I've ever set foot in a synagogue.'

'Everyone is welcome here,' the other woman said. She was shorter than Claire by several inches. In person her complexion appeared darker than it did on the screen, and her cheekbones seemed broader. 'Why are you here?' the woman who was both Isabella del Sueño and Zetta Vidonia Oroso demanded. 'What do you want?'

'I'm here to save your privacy. To protect your career.'

'What do you mean? Wait. We have to get away from this gang.' Zetta Vidonia Oroso turned away from Claire Delacroix and made her way rapidly to the front of the room. She reached into her purse and pulled out an envelope, which she handed to the bearded man. She handed a similar envelope to the boy. Then she put her arms around him and kissed him on the cheek.

The boy squirmed away.

Zetta Vidonia Oroso laughed, exchanged embraces with the boy's parents, and rejoined Claire Delacroix. 'All right, let's go.'

She led the way on foot to a near-by, modest house. She turned a key in the lock and let them in. From the front parlor Claire Delacroix could see into the dining room, where a cloth-covered table was laid with assorted refreshments. Leicester Jenkins was nowhere to be seen, but Claire Delacroix was confident that he would find them in due course.

'Sit, please,' Zetta Vidonia Oroso instructed. 'We have probably three quarters of an hour before they descend on the house. Here, in the easy chair, sit.'

Claire Delacroix complied.

'Now,' Zetta hissed, 'what's all this about saving me? This is America. Everyone is safe here. Talk.'

Claire Delacroix identified herself and explained that she was the assistant of the famous detective Akhenaton Beelzebub Chase.

'Stupid name,' Zetta said. 'Never heard of him. What does he want?'

'He's looking for you.'

'Why?'

Claire Delacroix recounted the visit from Captain Baxter. 'Dr. Chase found the invitation to Isaac Laudalino Fonseca's *bar mitzvah* that you left in Carmel. He translated the Hebrew. Apparently he couldn't translate the other portion of the invitation, but you can be sure that he'll turn up at the synagogue. He may be there already.'

Zetta Vidonia Oroso nodded angrily. 'That was the Ladino version. He wouldn't understand that. I'm surprised that he can read Hebrew.'

'His parents were both archaeologists. Dr. Chase is familiar with the ancient languages of the Middle East.'

'All right.' Zetta Vidonia Oroso stood up. 'Stay here,' she said. She walked into the other room, filled a tray and returned to the parlor. Her gesture indicated that she wanted Claire Delacroix to accept refreshment; Claire took a square of sponge cake and glass of wine. The wine was heavy and sweet; Claire sipped carefully.

'How much do you know?' the actress asked.

'I know what Louella Parsons told me at San Simeon. We were riding in Gary Cooper's Duesenberg and I think Louella was a little tipsy.'

'Probably not. Louella tells what she wants to tell.'

'Isn't she a notorious gossip columnist?' Claire asked.

Zetta shook her head. 'Everything in her column is fed to her by studio publicists. That's what she writes. But she has her sources, too. She knows a lot more than she writes, and everybody in Hollywood knows it. That's how she gets them to give her exclusives. They know what they don't want her to publish, so they keep her supplied with all the best gossip.'

She had brought sponge cake and wine for herself as well as for Claire. She dipped the cake into her glass and nibbled at the wine-soaked cake.

Claire watched and followed suit. The combination was tolerable.

'All right, Miss Delacroix, I still want to

'know what Louella told you about me.'

'She said you're not really Spanish at all. That the whole story about your being born in Seville of royal blood is all studio hokum. That you were serving drinks in Carmel when Eberhard Kasper discovered you. That he was looking for a replacement for Maria Gonsalves Escobar, he needed a beautiful young woman with an aristocratic Spanish pedigree and he spotted you.'

'And what was my real background?'

'That you were really a Jewish girl from Greenpoint in Brooklyn.'

Claire Delacroix wondered whether her hostess would respond with anger to this revelation, or with shock. Instead she burst into laughter.

'The first part of the story is true,' she conceded. 'Yes, I was tending bar in Carmel and Eberhard came in for a drink. He must have been hitting the other bars before he came into the place where I was working. I remember it well. The Sussex Downs, and that slimy little manager, Dismas Grey, always trying to put the make on the cocktail waitresses.

When I checked into the hotel last Friday I wondered if that little worm would recognize me. I hadn't used my real name when I worked there years ago, and he never thought of the girls as people anyway.'

'But what about your ancestors? What about Brooklyn?'

'I've never been there in my life,' Zetta said. 'I was born right here in Monterey. My family came from Mexico. Do you know who the *Portegizen* are, Claire?'

Claire shook her head. She looked at her watch. If the rest of the party were going to arrive from the synagogue forty-five minutes after Claire and Zetta reached the house, they were nearly due.

'The *Portegizen* are Portuguese Jews. When the Inquisition came to Iberia many Jews became Christians to save their lives. But a lot of us remained secret Jews. Yes, us. That's who I am. And a lot of *Portegizen* came to the New World. There are secret Jewish communities in Mexico, in Surinam, there are even Jewish-Indian communities in parts of this country.'

Claire shook her head. 'I never knew.'

'My blood is mixed,' Zetta said. 'I'm part *Portegize*, part Mexican Indian. I think there are some escaped slaves in my family tree, too. I'm a *marrano*, Claire. I'm a mongrel dog.' The look on her face was an inscrutable mixture of pride and fury.

'If word got out that I'm a mongrel my career would be over. I couldn't have it known that I was in Monterey to attend my little half-brother's *bar mitzvah*. My father died long ago and my mother remarried. Her second husband's name is Simao Timote Fonseca. My relatives know who I am but no one says a word. It's a family secret. The invitation to Mr. Hearst's party was just a lucky break for me. It got me away from Napa for a few days and nobody asked any questions. But I stupidly used that invitation for a bookmark. That's how you and this Chase learned about me, isn't it?'

Claire nodded.

The actress asked, 'Now what?'

'But you're so beautiful!' Claire exclaimed. 'How can you call yourself a mongrel,

Isabella?' She had slipped back into using the other woman's screen name.

'We mutts are always the strongest,' Zetta replied bitterly. 'We have all the best genes.'

The knocker on the front door sounded. Zetta started across the room.

'They're here,' the actress said. 'What are you going to do? You have to decide right now.'

Claire stood up. 'I'm an old friend,' she said. 'I'm your friend from Berkeley.'

Zetta nodded. She opened the door and the guests from the synagogue began to pour in, talking loudly, exchanging news and jokes, pressing toward the refreshments in the other room. Claire stood beside her easy chair. Zetta introduced her to relatives, to the young and the old, to the Orosos and the Fonsecas. She proudly introduced her half-brother, Isaac, the *bar mitzvah* boy.

Through the open front door there came the sound of an Indian motorcycle's four-cylinder engine. Claire Delacroix made her way to the doorway and saw Leicester Jenkins climbing from his two-wheeler. The familiar Hispano-Suiza drew to the curb behind the motorcycle and Abel Chase emerged from it.

★   ★   ★

An hour later a trio sat at a quiet table in a restaurant in Carmel-by-the-Sea. A light meal had been served, and at each place there stood a glass of wine. Conversation during the meal had been desultory, but as a waitress in antique style blouse and skirt cleared the dishes, Abel Chase spoke.

'I wish to thank you, Jenkins, for waiting at the synagogue and leading me to the Fonseca home. But now, please feel free to return to Berkeley. You will find something extra in your pay envelope this week.'

Jenkins nodded. 'Thank you, Dr. Chase.' He made a half-bow to Claire Delacroix and left the restaurant. A moment later the sound of the four-cylinder Indian motorcycle broke the tranquility of the *faux* English village, then faded quickly as Leicester Jenkins guided the machine toward the highway.

Abel Chase turned a stern visage toward Claire Delacroix. 'Please repeat for me the explanation you asked me to give Captain Baxter.'

'It's very simple,' Claire Delacroix replied, 'Señorita del Sueño spent Friday night at the Sussex Downs as she had indicated in her telephone call to San Simeon. If Mr. Hearst has any doubts about her veracity — which I very much doubt, but one can never tell — he can telephone the hotel and ask Dismas Grey for confirmation of that. When she awakened on Saturday she had a headache and symptoms of a bad cold. Rather than risk infecting Mr. Hearst's other guests, she decided simply to stay in Carmel until she was feeling better, then return to work in Napa.'

'Why didn't she telephone Hearst again and tell him she wasn't coming?'

'She just wasn't up to it. She was distraught at missing a San Simeon picnic and she couldn't bear to make the call.'

'Plausible enough, I suppose,' Abel Chase admitted.

192

'Of course Señorita del Sueño didn't use that name at the Sussex Downs. She registered as Zetta Vidonia Oroso. A sufficiently exotic name to be remembered, but one that would never make anyone suspect that she was really the famous Spanish beauty.'

'And the purpose of this elaborate ruse,' Abel Chase pursued, 'tell me that if you will, Miss Delacroix.'

Claire Delacroix did not like to fib, but she had undertaken an obligation to Zetta Vidonia Oroso. Her family history and her true identity were her own concern. Her studio proclaimed her to the world as Isabella del Sueño, and Isabella del Sueño she would be. Even Abel Chase would not know the full truth. Maybe someday, Claire Delacroix thought, a studio head would have the courage to make a picture revealing the whole story of the Oroso family and of the *Portegizen*.

Maybe someday. But until then, Zetta's secret would be known only to her family . . . and to Claire Delacroix.

'She must have felt a religious impulse,' Claire Delacroix told Abel Chase.

4

The Case of the Missing Man

Abel Chase's concentration was not interrupted by the insistent ringing of the great residence's door chimes, nor by the clatter of the massive, hand-cast door knocker. He continued to work on his response to the manuscript pages that lay before him on the huge, elaborately carven mahogany desk that dominated his private sanctum.

My Dear Fermi, Chase's letter opened in impeccable blackletter script, *I have before me the copy which you transmitted of the work which you and Madame Meitner seek to report, regarding your investigations into the possibility of obtaining vast amounts of energy by splitting the very atom of the element uranium.*

While your work is most promising, and I would by no means seek to discourage your pursuit of the subject, I must point out a few trivial errors, which I have detected in the underlying mathematics that you so thoughtfully included in your documentation.

The letter continued from there, of course in flawless and elegant Italian, which Chase would duplicate in the German language for the convenience of Lise Meitner, the world's leading female physicist, and, for that matter, one of the world's greatest scientific thinkers, regardless of gender.

But a knock on the door of Chase's study accomplished that which the telephone's signal had failed to do. The great polymath laid aside his silver-filigree pen and looked up.

'Enter,' he commanded.

The door swung back to reveal the sleek and willowy form of the always-elegant Claire Delacroix. This evening she wore a gown of shimmering midnight blue, her silvery blonde hair cascading in graceful waves over slim shoulders.

'A messenger from the telegraph station in Berkeley,' Claire Delacroix explained. 'I accepted the envelope and asked the boy to await an answer. He is standing outside beside his motorcycle now.'

'Very well,' Chase nodded. 'Please let me see the message at once.'

Claire Delacroix crossed the room, her silvery slippers seeming barely to touch the antique Bokhara carpet. She laid a slip of buff-colored paper on Abel Chase's desk.

Dr. Chase, it ran, *Captain Baxter of the San Francisco Police Department has recommended you to me. I face the most baffling case of my career, and would seek your assistance in the solution of this. I beseech you, sir, to come to Monterey at once. Spare no speed nor expense, if you please.*

The telegram was signed *Seamus Mahoney, Chief of Police, Monterey.*

Abel Chase folded the slip of paper and looked at Claire Delacroix. 'What do you make of this?' he inquired.

Claire Delacroix said, 'Apparently Cleland Baxter and Chief Mahoney are friends. Baxter must have told Mahoney about the way you solved the murder of

Imre Hunyadi at the Salamanca Theater in San Francisco. After that exploit, I shouldn't be surprised if a series of commissions arrived, starting with this one.'

Abel Chase pursed his lips. 'I fear you are right, Miss Delacroix. I managed to keep my role in the Hunyadi affair out of the press, but apparently there is a jungle telegraph among our police departments and word has begun to spread.'

He pushed his heavy chair away from the desk. 'Signor Fermi and Frau Meitner will have to wait, I fear. Perhaps a delay of a few days will not set their work back to any serious degree. Monterey is a charming fishing village. Its climate should be pleasant this time of year. Please ask Jenkins to fetch my suit coat and prepare yourself, Miss Delacroix, for a little jaunt.'

Claire Delacroix started for the door but Chase stopped her with a word. 'Oh — and send this reply to chief Mahoney: *Arriving in three hours. Please arrange lodging for myself, assistant, and chauffeur. Chase, Berkeley.* 'And give the telegraph boy a tip. Take the money from our household petty cash fund.'

With a brisk nod, Claire Delacroix exited the room. As she did so, Abel Chase lifted the onyx-and-gold telephone from his desk and placed a brief phone call.

Within minutes of dispatching the reply to Seamus Mahoney's telegram, Abel Chase, Claire Delacroix, and Jenkins had assembled in the foyer of Chase's mansion high in the Berkeley hills overlooking San Francisco Bay. A light fog had moved in through the Golden Gate but the sky overhead was clear and a myriad stars sparkled in their eternal places.

Chase and Claire Delacroix were clad in similar outfits of soft leather aviator's helmets and goggles, warm fleece-lined jackets, jodhpurs and boots. Jenkins had exchanged his butler's livery for a chauffeur's severe tunic and cap. He had brought with him the valises, which in this household were kept in readiness for use at any time, one for Dr. Chase, one for Miss Delacroix, and one for himself.

While Jenkins guided the Hispano-Suiza J12 with its immense 720 horsepower engine through the darkened hills that marked the dividing line between Alameda and Contra Costa Counties, Abel Chase and Claire Delacroix leaned back in the tonneau, discussing their newest enterprise.

'I am unfamiliar with this Mahoney,' Chase asserted. 'I trust that this case will prove of sufficient interest to justify my interrupting my important work.'

Claire Delacroix replied, 'Certainly Captain Baxter wouldn't have recommended you on anything less than a worthy case. But you know, Dr. Chase, I've always wondered how you and Clel Baxter became friends. I mean, you're one of the world's leading intellects, you are consulted by geniuses in every field from astronomy to medicine. The University of California has offered you any faculty post you might choose, and instead you only teach one or two courses each year to the most brilliant and promising of young minds. But when a police detective calls, you drop everything to lend him a hand.'

'It's a long story, Miss Delacroix,' Abel Chases paused, 'and not the most pleasant. You know that I served in the Great War, do you not?'

Claire Delacroix confirmed as much.

'It was at Ypres. I was a major at the time. Yes, this was shortly before my promotion to colonel. Captain Baxter — that is, the present Police Captain Baxter — was an enlisted soldier under my command — a corporal of infantry. The Hun mounted a gas attack upon us, and I saw Baxter's commander, a captain whose name I will not mention, funk it. Bullets were whizzing, you understand, waves of gas swept over the battlefield, the stench and filth of the trenches was disgusting. Truthfully, men were in hell on earth in that day.'

Even in the darkened tonneau of the Hispano-Suiza, Abel Chase's face showed the pain of recollection.

'Baxter's commander must have been drinking. I saw the man stumbling along the trench. A fragment of an enemy artillery round would have ricocheted off a buried rock; it was a peculiar, even freakish, display of the laws of physics. It bounded off the captain's helmet, knocking him to his knees.'

By now the Hispano-Suiza had descended from the hills and was speeding across the darkened city of Oakland under the skilled guidance of Jenkins.

'The captain brought up whatever rations and liquor he had consumed that day. He fouled his gas mask, which was all that had saved him from the enemy's poison. He pulled the mask from his face and cast it up, out of the trench and into No Man's Land. I saw him lurch to his feet, seize Baxter from behind and demand that he give him his mask.'

Chase shook his head. 'Never had I seen such a condemnable act of selfishness and cruelty. The captain pressed his sidearm against Baxter's skull and repeated his command. Baxter complied and the captain, shrieking with laughter, removed his helmet and pulled the gas mask over his own head.'

'Oh, horrid, horrid.' Claire Delacroix

took one of Abel Chase's hands in her own.

'I saw the look on Baxter's face. It was the look of a man who had done his duty, who had served his cause with honor, and who was now prepared to die uncomplainingly. I drew my own Colt and shot that captain through the skull. I had never before killed a man, and I felt neither guilt nor satisfaction, I knew only that I had done what I needed to do. But — '

A bitter smile creased Abel Chase's regular features. 'But,' he repeated, 'I had outsmarted myself. In executing that captain, that criminal and coward — I had ruined the gas mask he had taken from Baxter. Now there was only one thing to do. I removed my own gas mask and handed it to the soldier. Solemnly, he signed his gratitude and donned the mask as clouds of poison slowly enveloped us. That was the last thing I remembered, Miss Delacroix, until I awakened in a field hospital well behind the lines.'

Abel Chase slumped in his seat.

Claire Delacroix demanded breathlessly, 'What happened? How did you survive the gas attack? How did you get to the hospital? What became of the others involved?'

'Cleland Baxter is a modest man,' Abel Chase stated. 'It wasn't easy to get the story out of him, but in time he told all. As I lay in the bottom of that trench he threw a makeshift filter of wet burlap over my face. He fought through the battle, actually driving off wave after wave of attacking Hun. Then, as soon as the firing had quieted, he picked me up — I was quite unconscious by then — and carried me on his back to the first aid station. From there I was transferred to the field hospital. Of course my lungs were — well, I never returned to the Olympic trials which had been my goal before the war — but I survived, and am able to live a relatively normal life as long as I take care.'

'And when you got home from the war — what then?'

Abel Chase smiled, no longer bitterly. 'I discovered that Baxter was a native San Franciscan. Virtually a neighbor. We met, he expressed his desire to join the San

Francisco police force, and I was able to, well, place a word here and there. His career was made, nor has he ever done me other than proud.'

'A wonderful story,' Claire Delacroix responded. 'And you have come to his assistance whenever he has called, ever since.'

'I could do no other.'

The Hispano-Suiza had crossed the city of Oakland by now, and was rolling smoothly toward the municipal aerodrome. When it drew up before a fully appointed but discreetly unmarked private hangar, Jenkins pulled to a stop and raced to open the passenger door for Claire Delacroix. Once she had climbed from the tonneau Jenkins circled the Hispano-Suiza and opened the door for Abel Chase.

'Thank you, Jenkins. You may proceed by highway to Monterey. Miss Delacroix and I will await you there. If there is any question as to how you are to make contact with us, merely inquire of Captain Mahoney of the local police force. We will have spoken with him, at the very least, well before your arrival.'

Inside the hangar Abel Chase addressed a coverall-clad mechanic. 'I trust the gyroplane is ready for use, Maxon?'

'Yes, sir, Dr. Chase. Soon as you called, sir, I checked her out and gassed her up.' Maxon offered a mock-military salute, lifting his forefinger to the visor of his greasy cap. 'And a pleasure to see you, too, Miss Delacroix. As always.'

Democratically sharing the task with his mechanic, Abel Chase joined in rolling the Cierva C.8W from the hangar and onto the tarmac. With Claire Delacroix operating the controls and Abel Chase in the gyroplane's passenger seat, Maxon swung the Cierva's hand-carved propeller. Claire Delacroix hit the switch. The 220-horsepower Wright Whirlwind rotary caught and the gyroplane rolled forward. The new self-actuator set the gyroplane's rotor to spinning and the craft lifted from the tarmac in a nearly vertical trajectory.

As planned, Claire Delacroix headed due south from Oakland.

The night was clear and moonlight

gave the farmlands a ghostly radiance. There was enough traffic on the roadways, even at this hour, to make it possible to navigate by following the headlights and taillights of automobiles making their way to the rich agricultural lands surrounding Salinas, then swerving to the west toward the dark Pacific Ocean.

The roar of the air-cooled Wright engine precluded conversation as the gyroplane made its way overland. Claire Delacroix concentrated on observing the countryside and maintaining diligence over the aircraft's electrically illuminated instruments. The night air was chilly and the slipstream generated by the Cierva's airspeed — in excess of 100 miles per hour — was enough to assure that both pilot and passenger kept their goggles over their eyes and their fleece collars turned up.

While Claire Delacroix maneuvered the gyroplane skillfully through the California skies, Abel Chase found himself wondering what sort of case he would undertake once they landed in Monterey. The town was an old one, of course. The early history of Monterey was one of turmoil and rivalry dating back to the sixteenth century and involving the Spanish, the Portuguese, and the English. Names like Joao Rodrigues Cabrilho, Don Sebastian Vizcaino, and Sir Francis Drake collided in the early accounts. Hernan Cortes claimed to have 'discovered' California in 1535, totally discounting the Chumash, Ohlone and other peoples who had lived there from time immemorial. And Monterey itself was a city — or more accurately, a crude Spanish village — by 1770. It was for many years the capital city of old Alta California and the site where the Golden State's first constitution was written.

Now Monterey had slipped from controversy. It was a prosperous center for the catching and canning of sardines by the million, a seemingly endless supply of nature's bounty that filled the coffers of the wealthy owners of fishing fleets and canneries, and the lunch buckets of the brigades of workers who manned their vessels or stood on the endlessly rolling production lines of the canneries.

In due course the sturdy Cierva topped the peaks of the Santa Cruz Mountains. Moonlight glinted off the calm waters of Monterey Bay and the lights of City of Santa Cruz became visible to the north, those of the City of Monterey to the south. Claire Delacroix swung the little gyroplane into a graceful banking turn, hugging the foam-crested shoreline and heading toward their destination.

The moonlight showed them a vacant field near the Monterey Police Headquarters, and Claire Delacroix guided the Cierva in for a smooth landing on its grassy surface. Abel Chase climbed unassisted from the passenger seat and chivalrously offered his hand to Claire Delacroix.

They made their way to the squat headquarters building and startled a bulky uniformed desk sergeant out of his drowsy contemplation of a pulp magazine featuring a bloodthirsty ghoul on its lurid cover.

'My name is Akhenaton Beelzebub Chase. Please make contact with your chief and tell him that I am here.'

The sergeant dropped his magazine. A huge mug of half congealed coffee stood on one corner of his desk. He blinked at Abel Chase and Claire Delacroix, confusion and indecision following each other across his fleshy features. After a while he ran his fingers through his gray hair as if to restore circulation to his brain, then reached for the telephone.

Holding the earpiece in one hand he clutched the base of the phone in the other, clicking the fork up and down until there was a response from the operator. He muttered into the mouthpiece, waited, then spoke again.

He hung the earpiece back on the fork and returned the telephone to its corner of his desk. 'Chief Mahoney says he didn't expect yez until morning, sir. He says to make yez welcome and comfortable here, and he'll be right down as soon as he can pull his trousers on. Pardon me, Miss, I didn't think before I said that, I hope ye'll forgive it.'

Abel Chase and Claire Delacroix spent the next half hour drinking the Monterey

Police Department's coffee and eating its pastries while they awaited the arrival of Chief Mahoney. He arrived at last clad in dungarees and flannel workshirt, badly in need of a shave, his hair as gray as the sergeant's and looking as if he'd escaped a cyclone by the narrowest of margins.

'Please forgive me,' he gasped. 'I didn't expect you until noon tomorrow at the soonest. How in the world did you get here so quickly, if I may ask?'

Abel Chase deferred to Claire Delacroix, who led the chief to a window. She pointed to the Cierva gyroplane, visible now in silhouette against the bright night sky.

'You flew down in one of them things?' Mahoney exclaimed.

'Señor de la Cierva and his American associate, Mr. Pitcairn, have asked me to evaluate their gyroplane as to its technical qualities and its potential as a commercial product. Miss Delacroix and I decided to travel from Oakland by air as a test of the gyroplane's abilities. In fact it has performed flawlessly and with a few recommendations which I shall furnish to de la Cierva and Pitcairn, I am confident that a bright future awaits rotary winged aircraft.'

Giving the chief a moment to assimilate this information, Abel Chase resumed. 'But that is a matter for Miss Delacroix and myself to deal with after we return to Berkeley. For now, you will please conduct us to suitable lodgings. You have made arrangements, per my instructions? Good. And once we are settled in our quarters, I will ask you to fill us in on the remarkable case that has brought us all this distance.'

Mahoney conducted them to a Lafayette police cruiser. A uniformed officer, several decades younger and several degrees more alert than the desk sergeant they had encountered at headquarters, guided the cruiser over the hilly local streets, twin headlights picking out a picturesque mix of architecture suggestive of past centuries as well as the present day.

Shortly Abel Chase and Claire Delacroix were checked into a three-room suite at a comfortable establishment on Calle

Alvarado. Abel Chase selected a pleasant room furnished in antique woodcraft; Claire Delacroix settled in the second chamber, slightly the smaller but similarly appointed. Their personal belongings, they knew, were already *en route* from the mansion in the Berkeley hills, safely stowed in the Hispano Suiza and deftly directed by the skillful Jenkins.

They assembled in the sitting room along with Chief Mahoney. A sleepy desk clerk in the ground floor lobby personally delivered a tray of hot beverages and tiny sandwiches, placing it on a low table between a brocade-covered divan and a pair of matching wing chairs.

'Now,' Abel Chase began, sipping at a cup of frothy chocolate, 'Unburden yourself, Chief.'

Seamus Mahoney nodded vigorously, his gray thatch falling over his broad forehead. 'I called Captain Baxter about this because it has me totally baffled. The case came to me from our harbormaster, I should say harbormistress, Senhorita Johanna Cabrilho.'

'I take it that Senhorita Cabrilho is

related to the distinguished *familia* Cabrillo?' Abel Chase inquired.

'Indeed, sir. The Cabrillos or Cabrilhos were descended from Joao Rodrigues Cabrilho, a Portuguese Don. The name was later altered to the Spanish spelling, but Miss Cabrilho is a proud and strong-willed woman and she has returned to the original version of her family name.'

Mahoney leaned forward and lifted a sandwich from the tray.

He studied it and shook his head sadly. 'Would hardly fill a corner of an Irishman's belly, this little thing. Well, 'tis better than nothing, I say.' He swallowed the sandwich at a bite, then resumed. 'The harbormistress supervises all our marine activity, of course, including the present attempt to find the old Spanish galleon *Reina Ramona* and raise her gold. The *Ramona* sank in Monterey Bay well over two centuries ago, Dr. Chase, and of course there are more legends and fairy tales about the treasure and its guardians than you can shake a stick at. Most of our sardiners are Portugees, and you know how superstitious the Portugees can be,

213

sir! Pirates, skeletons, ghosts, there's no end.'

'But surely, Chief, you did not summon me to debunk a myth?'

'No, sir. What happened was this — well, Miss Cabrilho should be joining us momentarily and — ah, a knock!'

It was, indeed, Senhorita Johanna Cabrilho, harbormistress of the Monterey Bay. She was a tall woman of middle years, her glossy hair swept behind her, knotted and held in place by a metallic clasp. Her features were regular; her skin was olive and showed the signs of long exposure to the sun's rays. She wore a man's chambray work shirt, heavy trousers, boots, and a padded jacket which she doffed as she entered the room.

Chief Mahoney made introductions, then said, 'Johanna, Dr. Chase and Miss Delacroix are here to help us with the murder investigation.'

'What murder investigation?'

Abel Chase raised his eyebrows.

'The murder of the diver, Mr. Stimson, from the salvage ship *San Salvador*, of course.' Mahoney looked annoyed.

'We don't know that he was murdered,' Johanna Cabrilho snapped. 'We don't know that he's dead.'

Mahoney heaved a sigh made a helpless gesture. 'You see, Dr. Chase? I never heard of a female harbormaster before, and I hope I never do again. Beggin' your pardon, Johanna, but what else d'ye think could have happened to poor Stimson?'

Johanna Cabrilho shook her head. Her eyes were large and very dark. They shone with intelligence and with an inner strength.

'We know that the salvage company has a pretty good idea where the *Reina Ramona* lies. A few objects have washed up on the shore. If the galleon had fallen into the trench there's no way that ordinary currents could lift anything and bring it to shore, and if the ship lay on the north side of the trench nothing would find its way to our beaches, it would wash ashore on the Santa Cruz side of the bay. That much is simple.'

Abel Chase nodded his understanding.

'So Stimson went down to search for the wreck,' Johanna Cabrilho went on.

'His diving suit was checked out before he left the deck of the *San Salvador*. His air hose and hoist line were connected. He climbed over the ship's railing and was lowered into the bay. Everything was normal.'

'Aye,' Chief Mahoney interrupted, 'and then what happened, eh?' He took another sandwich from the tray, tore off a corner with large teeth and waited for her answer.

'Right, Chief.' Johanna Cabrilho was unflapped. 'Stimson was on the bottom for a long time. They were starting to worry about him on deck. He didn't signal and he didn't respond to their signals so they hoisted him back up, or tried to. All they got back was an empty diving suit.'

'An empty suit!' Claire Delacroix exclaimed. 'Was the suit damaged? Was there any sign of accident or foul play?'

Johanna Cabrilho shook her head. 'Nothing. The suit was undamaged. The helmet was still firmly locked to the collar. The boots and their lead weights were even attached to the legs of the suit. Stimson had simply vanished.'

Abel Chase had sat during the Johanna Cabrilho's narrative and the comments of the others in the room with a look of rapt concentration on his features. Claire Delacroix knew that look, and having assisted Abel Chase in unraveling some of his most baffling mysteries, she was not surprised when he bounced to his feet and began to pace, back and forth, across the sitting room.

Outside the hotel the sky was beginning to lighten with the approach of dawn. In the harbor, Portuguese fisherman would already be on their boats, preparing to sail onto the bay and the ocean beyond and bring in the day's haul of silver sardines, the flashing shining dollars that supported the economy of the town and its environs.

Abel Chase halted and gazed sharply at the others.

'If my lungs would permit, I would be tempted to suit up myself and follow Stimson's trail. But the Kaiser's poison gas has made that a limited option for me. There will be other ways to pursue this case.'

'Ye don't think, then, that some sea spirit got Stimson?' Mahoney queried.

'You did not seem so credulous a few minutes ago, Chief.'

'Nor am I, sir. But — what other explanation is there, do ye think?'

'I do not know, that I will confess. But then, if one knew the answer to a puzzle at the outset, where would lie the challenge, where the pleasure of finding the solution? No, Chief Mahoney, I do not know where Mr. Stimson went, but I agree with Miss Cabrilho that we cannot yet assume his demise. No indeed. And,' he smiled, 'that adds to the piquancy of the situation.'

The sky behind Abel Chase had assumed a salmon pinkness now. To those seated opposite him he presented a dramatic silhouette, tall and almost unnaturally slim. Of this he was not unaware. It was time for him to assert control of the situation.

'Tell me, Miss Cabrilho, where is Mr. Stimson? Surely you have a theory.'

The harbormistress shook her head. 'I'm afraid not, sir. I have the word of Captain Maginnis of the *San Salvador* and of his dive master, Mr. Lawton, as to what happened. I inspected their ship and the diving apparatus. I saw the empty suit. But I had never met Mr. Stimson and I have no idea as to his fate. For all I know there never was a Mr. Stimson. But assuming that there was, I suspect there may have been a crime, which is why I brought Chief Mahoney into the case.'

Abel Chase lowered his face and grasped his chin between forefinger and thumb, his expression one of intense concentration. 'I shall need to examine this famous empty diving suit, as soon as possible. And of course question the captain and dive master. Further, Chief Mahoney — Chief!'

Mahoney lowered the coffee and sandwich that had held his concentration. 'Sir?'

'I'll need to know what, if anything, your own efforts have produced.'

Before Mahoney could respond the

conference was interrupted by a diffident knock at the door. Recognizing its pattern, Claire Delacroix rose and admitted the newcomer. Abel Chase's *major domo* and man of all trades entered the sitting room. He still wore his midnight blue chauffeur's costume. 'The Hispano is garaged and the management is sending your luggage up, sir. As soon as it arrives I shall attend to your belongings, Dr. Chase.'

He turned toward Chase's assistant with the suggestion of a bow. 'May I assume that Miss Delacroix prefers to tend to her own belongings.'

Claire Delacroix nodded.

'In that case,' Abel Chase announced, 'this meeting is adjourned. I suggest that we reassemble tomorrow at Miss Cabrilho's office. Will ten o'clock be acceptable to all? Very well then, I thank you for your assistance.'

★ ★ ★

By midmorning a light mist was all that remained of the fog that had shrouded

Monterey Bay during the night. Abel Chase and Claire Delacroix, clad in rough trousers and heavy shirts, had commandeered a police cruiser for transportation to the wharf where Johanna Cabrilho's office was located. The office itself consisted of little more than a wooden shack furnished with an extensive array of marine charts, tide tables, ephemera and volumes of data on seafaring concerns. A huge representation of Monterey Bay covered much of one wall.

A battered coffee pot stood precariously balanced on a crude hotplate.

Johanna Cabrilho sat behind a scratched and battered desk, a scarred telephone at her elbow. Chief Mahoney stood near the hotplate, a cup of coffee steaming in one hand, a half-consumed pastry in the other.

In short order Johanna Cabrilho was standing before the big wall chart explaining the layout of the bay. Unlike San Francisco Bay a hundred miles to the north with its narrow channel, the famous Golden Gate, Monterey Bay opened to the Pacific in a broad, cup-shaped configuration. The great trench that divided the bay was of course invisible from the shore but was marked prominently on the chart.

An errant ray of morning sunlight had seemingly been caught in Johanna Cabrilho's thick black hair, making it glow like dark flame.

'Here is the *San Salvador*.' The harbormistress indicated an offshore location. 'Here is the area where Captain Maginnis thinks *La Reina Ramona* went down in 1598. Or, more accurately, where he thinks it was carried by two hundred and thirty-six years worth of tides and storms. In fact, the ship probably went down on the other side of the trench. There must have been a huge swell to carry it across the trench. If it had ever dropped into the fissure it would never have come back up, you can bet on that. But every so often some little artifact washes up here on the beach or turns up in a sardine net, so we know it's somewhere around here, and not too deep.'

'How certain is Captain Maginnis that

this galleon is where he thinks it is? Flotsam is always turning up, is it not? Are there records, possibly in Spain, to support this claim?'

'You can find as many stories as you want,' Seamus Mahoney volunteered. He picked a fragment of sugar pastry off his uniform tunic and popped it into his mouth. 'You ask some of the Chinee around here, they'll tell you that a junk full o' treasure went down in the bay before the Spanish ever got to California.'

He refilled his coffee mug from Johanna Cabrilho's battered pot.

'And they have some pieces of jade and some lovely porcelain to show, too.' He swigged from his mug, wiped his mouth, then resumed, speaking around another bite of pastry. 'But it don't prove there's a Chinee treasure ship down there any more as a battered-in helmet or a bent doubloon proves there's a galleon under the bay.'

Claire Delacroix turned back from the window. 'It might be useful, perhaps, were we made aware of any abnormal activity taking place in the bay. Is there, Miss Cabrilho?'

'Just the usual,' Johanna Cabrilho furnished. 'The sardine fleets are out. There are a few pleasure craft on the bay. And of course Captain Maginnis and Mister Lawton and their crew on the *San Salvador*. There's no treasure diving going on, you understand. As soon as I learned about the disappearance of the diver Stimson, I ordered them to suspend all diving.'

'How did they take that?'

Johanna Cabrilho offered a wry grin. 'Mad as a couple of wet hens. And when I ordered them to stay at anchor and keep their crew on board they were fit to be tied. I don't know how long I can detain them, in fact. If they were on the high seas there wouldn't be anything I could do, Captain Maginnis would be King Maginnis. But as long as they're in the bay, the harbormaster outranks even the master of a ship. But we'll need to resolve this quickly or I'll have to release them.'

'That's all then?'

'Just about. And of course there are always a few odd characters around these parts. Puritans in Pacific Grove, mystics and nudists in Carmel. Here in Monterey we mainly have working men — and some working girls to keep them happy. And those peculiar Italians down the beach. Things are usually pretty quiet around here.'

'So ye see,' Seamus Mahoney started, but Abel Chase whirled on Johanna Cabrilho, shutting the police chief off with a single sharp gesture.

'What peculiar Italians?'

Johanna Cabrilho laughed. 'A trio of eccentrics. What are their names, I have them somewhere here.' She shuffled through some papers on her desk. 'Here it is. DiMeo, Cabrini, Spelta. They came into my office when they arrived in town, wanted to know how to get a license, wanted to know who got the bribe money and how much it should be. Apparently under the *Fascisti* in Italy you need a permit to do anything including kissing your wife. And when you apply for it you have to bribe everybody or you wind up with a bloody nose and a stern warning not to make trouble.'

She dropped the paper on her desk, then continued.

'All they want to do is go swimming. They're working on a new kind of swimsuit and some new breathing gadgets. I don't see why they need a license to go swimming. They're right down the way here, wave and whistle at me every time they see me. I think they were amazed to see a woman in this job. Or any job except maybe a nurse or a cook.'

Abel Chase said, 'I take it you have the use of a launch.'

'I do.'

'I wish to visit the *San Salvador*. Chief Mahoney, there will be no further need for your services at this time and I believe you have other duties to attend to. Miss Delacroix, if you will be so kind as to accompany Miss Cabrilho and myself and take notes, thank you.'

Moments later they were settled in the motor launch that was assigned to the harbormaster's office, making their way into the bay toward the anchored salvage ship. Johanna Cabrilho guided the launch to settle smoothly alongside the *San Salvador*. A sailor from the salvage ship took a line and lashed the launch securely while Abel Chase, Claire Delacroix, and Johanna Cabrilho were guided to the captain's quarters.

* ★ ★ ★

Captain Maginnis might have studied for his role. The portion of his face not covered by his gray-flecked beard was weather-beaten and leathery; he wore a disreputable version of an officer's jacket and held a bulldog pipe clenched in his teeth.

As soon as the newcomers entered his cabin he leaped to his feet. Ignoring Abel Chase and Claire Delacroix he growled, 'Well, Miss Lady Habormaster Ma'am, I hope you've come to release me from this peculiar prison you've had me in since yesterday.'

'I'm afraid not quite yet, Captain. As soon as we solve this mystery I'll be happy to release you.'

Maginnis growled again. 'You know, we were hired to do this job. I have to run my ship and pay my crew. Every hour costs me money, Miss Cabrilho.'

'Your cooperation will help me, Captain, and then I can lift my order. Now, please give Dr. Chase and Miss Delacroix the same cooperation you would give to me. And, Dr. Chase, Miss Delacroix, if you will excuse me, I'll take the launch and go back to work. I'm sure Captain Maginnis will send you ashore in a dinghy when you're ready to go.'

Claire Delacroix said, 'Dr. Chase, you don't really need me to take notes. I'd like to go back ashore if you don't mind.'

Abel Chase looked startled but he assented. Captain Maginnis accompanied them back on deck. Johanna Cabrilho and Claire Delacroix clambered back aboard the harbormistress's launch and returned to the shore.

On board the *San Salvador* Abel Chase expected to converse with Captain Maginnis and Mister Lawton, but Maginnis uttered an oath and stalked away. He halted, facing a nearby group of sailors, and began berating them in incomprehensible nautical terms.

Lawton leaned toward Abel Chase. 'Don't mind the captain, sir. He likes to run his ship his own way and he doesn't like giving in to anyone. Least of all to a woman, although I'll say that your harbormistress here is about as easy to take as any woman I've ever met. And your Miss Delacroix — '

'If you don't mind, Mister Lawton, I am here to conduct an investigation, not to engage in idle chit-chat.'

The dive master straightened. 'All right, sir. If that's the way it is, ask your questions and let's finish our palaver.'

'Very well. Now, Mister Lawton, where was the *San Salvador* when the unfortunate incident took place?'

'Right where she is at this moment, sir. The sardine boats go out and they come back in, but the *San Salvador* hasn't moved a fathom since Mr. Simpson went down and didn't come back up.'

'And where do you believe the wreck of *La Reina Ramona* to lie?'

Lawton pointed at his boots. 'There she lies, straight down, some sixty feet below us. If the bay were clear water you could see her from *San Salvador's* deck. But Monterey Bay is a lively body of water. Streams feed into the bay, the tides flow and ebb, we've got wave action. It's a lovely spot, but it doesn't make for clear water and easy seeing. No, sir.'

'But you are convinced that it's the *Reina* down there and not a treasure ship from China?'

Lawton shrugged. 'The Chinee folk, they're pretty insistent, that I'll say. I guess they're entitled to believe whatever they want, until we know for sure.'

Abel Chase said, 'I wish to see the suit Stimson wore for his final dive.'

Lawton led the investigator to a storage locker. Its rusty iron hinges screamed as he pulled the door open. 'Here it is, sir.'

In fact the suit itself, of heavy rubberized canvas, was separate from the diving helmet. The massive helmet was made of rigid copper. It was fitted with windows of thick glass at either side. The window at the front of the helmet was hinged. Fittings permitted the attachment of an air hose at the top of the helmet. Its bottom was flanged and grooved to provide a firm lock to the brass collar of the canvas diving suit.

'You see, sir?' Lawton set the helmet carefully on the *San Salvador's* wooden deck.

'Does the diver wear boots?'

'Leaded shoes. We have to control the buoyancy. We don't want him floating around down there and we don't want him to turn upside down.'

Abel Chase rubbed his jaw between thumb and forefinger. 'Where are the shoes Stimson wore?'

The dive master shrugged massive, blue-clad shoulders. 'Wherever Mister Stimson is. Maybe he still has them. Or maybe they're still down there.' He gestured downward. 'They're made so the diver can jettison them if he needs an emergency release. That's a last hope, you see. If he releases his shoes he'll bob to the surface like a cork. Like as not

231

he'll wind up with nitrogen bubbles in his joints. There are cripples who've done that. Men have even died of it. And if you live through it you'll like as not wind up with a pain-wracked, twisted body. That's why we call it the bends. That's why any diver would rather wait for us to bring him up slowly, pause now and then, let those bubbles dissipate. Usually we like to use a diving platform, but we don't have one on this job so we're doing without.'

Chase nodded his understanding. He lifted the canvas suit.

Even without the massive helmet it was surprisingly heavy. He sniffed. It had a musty, unpleasant smell. He peered inside, ran his hands inside the suit. 'It's dry,' he exclaimed.

'Yes, it is.'

'Was it dry when you brought it up?'

'Nope. That's the strange part. Helmet was dry — full of air. Suit was full of water. We dried it out to keep it clean. Leave a suit wet, especially with brine or brackish, you've got a nasty, sticky mess next time you use it.' Lawton began stowing the diving suit in its locker. 'You're through with it, sir?'

Absently, Chase gave his assent. The suit was full of water when it came back up, he thought, yet the helmet was dry and full of air. More strangeness. Had he strong lungs he would have insisted on donning the suit and tracing Stimson's final descent, but he knew that such an enterprise now would be dangerous for him, possibly fatal. Still, this was an important aspect of his investigation. A bachelor with few close relationships, he might solve this mystery by retracing Stimson's route.

Undecided, he asked a further question.

'How can a man see at the bottom of the bay?'

'Only with the greatest of difficulty.' Lawton grinned at his own witticism. 'It's pitch black down there. A diver can carry an electric torch.'

He produced one from the suit locker.

'You see, it's much like an ordinary flashlight, but of course it has to be waterproof. And it has to be built to take

233

the pressure or it would be crushed in a second.'

He handed the torch to Abel Chase who switched it on and studied its powerful beam, then returned it to Lawton.

'I will go to the floor of the bay,' Abel Chase announced, 'and find out what happened to Mr. Stimson. Please assist me in donning this diving suit.'

'Sir!' the dive master exploded the word. 'You need certification to dive. You need training. You can't just climb into the suit and dive. That's crazy. That could be suicide.'

'I am acting in behalf of the Monterey Police Department. This is a criminal investigation, Mr. Lawton. Please assist me.'

* * *

At the harbormaster's shack Johanna Cabrilho invited Claire Delacroix to share the lunch of coffee and chicken sandwiches that she produced from a hidden half-size ice box. The coffee by now was bracingly strong albeit stale.

The two women were a study in contrasts. One was tall and gracefully slim with delicate features, platinum hair and pale blue eyes; the other, sturdily built with almost mannish shoulders, a chiseled nose and chin, broad cheekbones and flashing black eyes. Yet there was the shared strength and understanding between them of two women who knew what it meant to stand on their own feet and make their own ways in a man's world.

Claire Delacroix sat on a battered wooden chair opposite Johanna Cabrilho's equally battered desk. The harbormistress leaned back in a chair of her own, legs stretched out before her, knees crossed, scuffed boots on the desktop.

'All right,' Johanna Cabrilho queried, 'now that the geniuses are out of earshot, what do you think, sister?'

'You would know better than I,' Claire Delacroix answered. 'You know the bay, you've been on the *San Salvador*. Did you know this man Stimson?'

'Never laid eyes on him.'

'Do you really think he's alive?'

Johanna Cabrilho shrugged and grunted something that sounded like, 'I dunno.'

'Not even an educated guess? What could have happened to him?'

The woman shrugged again.

'I can't tell you that, sister, but I'll tell you this much.' The harbormistress laid a half-eaten sandwich on a scrap of waxed paper. She downed a hefty swig of strong coffee. She grimaced. 'Phew! That'll put hair on your chest!' She wiped her mouth. 'I'll tell you this much,' she repeated, 'there's probably a treasure down there sure enough. Whether it's Spanish or Chinese I can't tell you. The white people want it to be Spanish and the Chinese want it to be Chinese and they both have enough jugs and plates and knives and trinkets to make a pretty good case.'

She sat up straight, pulling her feet off her desk and setting them on the rough-hewn floor with a crash. 'But I'll tell you this much, sister, where there's a treasure there are going to be greedy men to fight over it. And where you get that you're likely to get some fool who's willing to kill another fool to get his share of the wealth!'

Claire Delacroix swallowed a morsel of chicken sandwich and a sip of coffee. She lowered the remnants of her meal to the desk. 'What about other boats in the bay?'

Johanna Cabrilho looked at her. 'What about 'em?'

'Could Stimson have transferred to another boat?'

Johanna Cabrilho pondered that for a while. 'No.' She shook her head. 'Well, not impossible at that. It's an interesting notion. And in fact there was a trawler hovering near the *San Salvador* when she first cast anchor offshore. But she doesn't seem to be doing anything, just sitting in the bay. Now, what was her name?'

She shuffled papers on her desk, picked up the telephone and found the paper she was looking for. '*Maria Elena*. Captain Moretti. Berthed in Monterey. But even if Stimson wanted to transfer from *San Salvador* to *Maria Elena* he'd have had to — what? Dive from *San Salvador* and switch diving suits under sixty feet of water. Then they'd have to raise him onto *Maria Elena*. Can't be done.'

Claire Delacroix pursed her lips in concentration. After a moment she said, 'Where are those Italians you mentioned before we went out to the *San Salvador*?'

'Last I knew they were on the beach down at Lover's Point. Just south of the big cannery, toward Pacific Grove. Probably still there, they seemed to be settling in for a stay.'

'Is that within walking distance?'

'Easily.'

Claire Delacroix nodded thoughtfully, then rose to her feet. 'May I use your telephone, Miss Cabrilho?'

Johanna Cabrilho shrugged. 'Help yourself.'

Claire Delacroix placed a call, spoke briefly, then hung the earpiece back on its hook. She thanked Johanna Cabrilho and left the harbormaster's shack.

Outside the shack the sun was blazing down. The bay reflected the bright blue of the sky. A breeze blew gently offshore, lifting Claire Delacroix's silvery hair with invisible fingers.

She headed toward Pacific Grove, passing huge buildings filled with sweating rough-handed and rough-spoken workers, many of them women, and massive machinery that turned fresh-caught sea life into meals that would feed thousands — including Monterey fishermen and cannery workers and their families. The smell of fish and the oil used to pack them was overwhelming.

Whistles and catcalls assailed Claire Delacroix as she hurried along Cannery Row. She was relieved to pass the last cannery and cross the city line into Pacific Grove. She found Lover's Point quickly enough, then clambered down a rocky decline marked with tussocks of tough sea-grass to reach the sandy shore.

The Italians' encampment was easily identified. They had managed somehow to maneuver a two-wheeled metal automobile trailer onto the beach, carefully parking it above the high tide line. Remnants of a campfire were visible not far from the unusual, tear-drop shaped trailer. Loud voices emerged from the trailer, raised in song with gusto if not with talent. There was even the sound of an out-of-tune concertina.

Prior to approaching the trailer, Claire Delacroix made her way to the shore. From here she had a clear view of the bay, save for a small area cut off by the last large building on Cannery Row. Johanna Cabrilho's office shack was hidden but the *San Salvador* stood forlorn some eighty or hundred yards offshore. Practically at her feet a rowboat stood, pulled out of the bay's gentle wavelets but moored to a heavy rock to prevent its drifting away with a high tide.

Claire Delacroix gazed at the bay's innocent-looking surface. A man had left *San Salvador's* deck wearing a bulky diving suit and the suit had been hoisted back on deck *sans* occupant. The diver Stimson was missing. Where was the missing man?

Baffled, Claire Delacroix turned back to the trailer and knocked on its door.

The concertina music and the singing stopped. There were sounds of scrambling and objects being put away.

The door swung open and Claire Delacroix confronted the reincarnation of Rudolph Valentino.

'*Signorina?*'

Claire let out her breath. No, it wasn't Valentino, of course not. The sheik was not in Pacific Grove, California, standing in the doorway of a cramped trailer, he was safely in his tomb in Forest Lawn. This man was one of the Italian visitors who had asked Johanna Cabrilho about a swimming license.

'*Signorina?*' the man repeated. From behind him, Claire Delacroix could hear his companions moving around.

'I work for a marine equipment company,' Claire improvised.

She reached into a pocket of her warm shirt and withdrew a business card. It read, *Maxon, Jenkins and Chase, Incorporated. Miss Claire Delacroix, Special Representative*. Carefully lacking in specifics, the card could be used in practically any situation.

'I'd like to talk with you about advances in diving gear.' The Valentino look-alike grinned broadly. He had a

241

wonderful smile and splendid teeth.

'Thank you so much,' he replied. He spoke English well but with a heavy accent. 'But we have our own gear, we brought our own gear from home. From Palermo. You know Palermo, in Italy, the most beautiful country.'

Claire offered her best smile in return. 'I was in Palermo a few years ago. A beautiful city, yes. But I did not come to sell you equipment. May I please come in? Maxon, Jenkins and Chase have heard of your work and are intrigued by it. They asked me to make contact with you.'

After a moment's hesitation the look-alike stood aside.

When Claire Delacroix started to climb into the trailer he took her hand and helped her in.

'Francesco DiMeo,' he identified him-self. 'And my, ah, friends and, yes, colleagues. This is Rocco Cabrini. This is Vittorio Spelta.' He turned toward the other men. '*La Signorina* Delacroix.'

While he let fly a stream of rapid-fire Italian, Claire got a look at the others.

Rocco Cabrini was heavy-set, with a

full head of black curls and a giant moustache. He wore a simple shirt and canvas khaki trousers. Vittorio Spelta gave off waves of radiance. Slim and surprisingly reserved, he actually bowed over Claire's hand.

'Would the *signorina* like, ah, a glass of wine and some *panne*, eh, bread and, eh, cheese?'

He seemed delighted with himself for getting the question out and quite crushed when Claire declined the offer.

'What I would like to do,' Claire said, 'is discuss the possibility of our firm's taking an American license to manufacture and sell your new diving equipment.'

Following a brief exchange among the Italians, DiMeo shook his head. 'I do not know what equipment the *signorina* means.'

The answer was no surprise to Claire. 'Is this your own invention, just the three of you? Or are you working for a company in your homeland, or for the Italian government?'

DiMeo indicated that he didn't understand the question. His English skills seemed to be slipping as the conversation progressed.

'If you are employees, surely you will receive a bonus from your employer if you bring in a contract from Maxon, Jenkins, and Chase. In fact, our company will pay you a very substantial bonus. And if this is your own invention, you will be rich men, I can assure you.'

There was a silence in the trailer, followed by an exchange of loud words and vigorous gestures among the three Italians. Then the dignified Vittorio Spelta took charge.

'If the *signorina* will step outside, *per favore*, just *uno minuto*.'

Claire took a step backwards, out of the trailer, onto the hard-packed sand.

Vittorio Spelta nodded, almost bowed, smiled, said, '*Mille grazi*,' and pulled the door shut.

This time the voices were not raised in song, nor was there any concertina music.

The door to the trailer swung open.

Francisco DiMeo said, 'Perhaps the *signorina* would like to meet in better surroundings than these. You have an office in this city, yes?'

Think fast, Claire Delacroix!

'First I will need to evaluate your gear, Signor DiMeo.'

DiMeo pulled his head inside the trailer and slammed the door.

More exchanges in loud Italian.

More clattering.

The door swung open.

Rocco Cabrini clambered out, or perhaps it was a new species of amphibian or maybe a man from another planet garbed to survive on Earth. He wore a strange outfit of black rubber, stretched tightly over his rotund torso. Instead of boots or shoes he wore a flat rubber device on each foot, splayed and ribbed like the foot of a frog. In one hand he carried a spear.

He wore a rubbery cap or hood that covered his thick hair but left his face exposed. He grinned sheepishly at Claire, then fitted a mouthpiece in place. Finally he pulled a pair of glass goggles into place. He bowed humorously. He looked more than a little like Oliver Hardy.

When he turned toward the bay, Claire

saw a cylindrical tank fastened to his back looking not unlike an oxygen supply as used in the more advanced hospitals. He waddled toward the bay, feet splayed, head bobbing. Even as she watched Cabrini, transfixed, Claire was aware of DiMeo and Spelta emerging from the trailer and standing quietly a few paces from her.

When Rocco Cabrini reached the water's edge he paused to adjust his mouthpiece, then took a first careful step into the bay. He waded until he was waist deep, pulled his waistband open as if to fill his rubbery suit with water, then turned back to wave his spear in a gesture of mock fierceness. Then he resumed his slow march.

With a motion suggestive of a swooping gull he dipped his head and shoulders into the water, then disappeared altogether beneath the surface.

Claire waited for a sign of Cabrini's whereabouts. After a few seconds she thought she might have seen a cluster of bubbles break the surface, but she could not be sure. If Cabrini's black rubber costume with its goggles and air tank and frog's feet was a new kind of diving suit, it was the strangest one that she had ever seen.

She sensed another presence and turned to confront Francesco DiMeo.

'The *signorina* would be warmer in the trailer. Or perhaps she would enjoy some refreshment.' He gestured. 'There are good restaurants nearby. A glass of wine, perhaps *un piato di cioppino*?'

Claire smiled. The prospect of wine and a delicious Italian fish stew with a man who looked like Rudolph Valentino was deeply tempting. The least she could do was try out her few words of Italian in return.

'*Molto grazi, signore, per no.*' That was about her limit.

'How long will *Signor* Cabrini be gone?'

'Not long.' DiMeo looked crestfallen. 'This is just *una dimonstrazione*, a what do you call, demonstration.'

'I don't see much.'

'Soon, soon, *Signorina* Delacroix.'

And shortly, the bulbous form of Rocco

Cabrini emerged from the brackish water of the bay. At first only his head, a black silhouette against the blue-green, then his shoulders and then his torso. He raised the absurd spear and to Claire's surprise a good-sized bass was impaled on it.

Moments later Cabrini stood before Claire Delacroix and Francesco DiMeo, frog's feet and all, dripping onto the pale sand. DiMeo nodded approvingly at the bass. '*Banchetto per tutti*,' he pronounced. 'Ah, dinner — *si?* — yes? — dinner for the everybody.'

Cabrini removed his frog's feet and walked into the trailer in a more dignified manner.

'What does the *signorina* think?' DiMeo asked.

'Very impressive.' She paused. 'But of course I didn't see very much.'

'*Signorina*, what more do you wish to see? Surely your company — tell me again its name, *per favore*.'

'Maxon, Jenkins and Chase, Incorporated.'

Maxon, Jenkins and Chase, *si*, it is strange that I do not know of them, but for that I apologize. But the *signorina* has seen *Signor* Cabrini demonstrate our new *produtto* — our product. You wish to enter into negotiations for a license. You said as much, is it not so?'

'I would like to try the gear myself. That way I will have a better idea of its comfort and usefulness. May I try it out?'

DiMeo flushed. 'I am so sorry, *signorina*, we have only the three suits. We have no extra suit for you to use.'

'I could borrow one, don't you think? Your *Signor* Spelta is a very slim man. I would think his suit would fit me.'

'Vittorio?'

'Yes.' Claire nodded.

'Hmm, Vittorio. But it is dangerous, the diving. The *signorina* knows how to dive? But even so, our new equipment is completely different. You need to learn how to use it.'

'You could teach me. I don't need to be an expert, just to try it out and get a general idea of how it works.'

DiMeo spent a while considering that. Finally he said, 'I will ask Vittorio if he will lend you his suit. Please to await me here, *signorina.*'

He disappeared into the trailer, following which the sounds of overlapping, excited, Italian voices were heard.

Finally the trailer door swung open.

Francesco DiMeo said, 'If the *signorina* is certain . . . '

Claire assured him. He gestured her into the trailer. Rocco Cabrini had changed back to dry clothing. Vittorio Spelta handed her a rubber diving suit, blushing with embarrassment as he did so. The Italians waited on the beach.

When Claire emerged she was clad in the black rubber garment. Even though it was dry it had a musty odor and a clammy feel against her skin. The three Italians competed to show her how to use the absurd frog's feet and how to don the tight rubber hood. It was hardly different from a swim cap.

Rocco Cabrini strapped a heavy air tank to her back and showed her how to use the breathing apparatus. Francesco DiMeo cautioned her. '*Signorina*, when you get into the water you must let a

— how to say this — a layer of water into the suit. You see? Otherwise, is too cold. But you keep a layer of water, ah, *imprigionato*, ah, imprisoned inside the suit. It grows warm from the heat of the body and you stay altogether happy, all warm.'

A very different system indeed from the traditional diving suit. Not that Claire was an expert, or had even used a diving suit. But she knew that the helmet stayed dry, and she assumed that the suit itself did the same. And air was pumped from the ship's deck; with the Italians' system the diver carried her own air with her.

Shy, gentlemanly Vittorio Spelta handed her an oddly shaped electric torch, then indicated that she could hook it to the waistband of her suit and keep both hands free. She flicked it on and off and thanked him, then attached the torch as Spelta had pantomimed.

Spelta blushed.

'Please, *signorina*,' DiMeo said, 'stay close. Do not go far or deep. The diving, it is dangerous.'

Claire started toward the water line.

Walking with the frog's feet was difficult, clumsy, but in a moment she was ankle deep in the brackish water. The bottom was smooth here and it was actually easier to walk now with the clumsy feet than it had been on the beach.

When the water passed Claire's waist she stopped and filled the lower half of her rubber suit. When she was neck deep she paused again and filled the upper half. The suit was flexible but even so there was not room for very much water in it. It was very cold.

She pulled her goggles into place, turned and waved to the trio of Italians standing on the beach. Genial DiMeo grinned and returned the gesture; rotund Cabrini nodded; shy Spelta blushed.

Claire imitated the move she had seen Cabrini make at the beginning of his demonstration dive. Cold bay water closed over her head. The breathing apparatus worked perfectly. The water inside her suit no longer felt chilled; in fact she was hardly aware of it.

She was in shallow water. With her goggles in place she was able to see clearly without the aid of the torch. She had entered another world: cool, green, tranquil.

As she swam she realized that the frog's feet were helping her to move forward. Rather than follow the conformation of the bay bottom she swam levelly. When she turned her head she could see the bright Pacific sun blazing above. There were no boats nearby.

She broke water and looked around. *San Salvador* rode at anchor ahead of her and to her right, to the northwest. She estimated her distance to the salvage craft. Under normal circumstances she realized that swimming to the *San Salvador* would stretch her endurance to the limit, but with the help of the frog's feet, and possibly the streamlined contours and smooth skin of the rubber suit, she was moving faster and more easily through the water than she ever had before.

Too bad, she mused, that there was no such firm as Maxon, Jenkins and Chase. A North American license to market the Italians' diving system would be worth having. But she had other and more immediate concerns to occupy her.

She approached the stern of *San Salvador*.

She raised her head above water and saw the diving gear on *San Salvador's* deck. A lifeline hung from the winch and an air hose from the pump. Someone was diving. Had Johanna Cabrilho lifted her order against further dives? If not, Captain Maginnis was risking a fat fine, possibly the loss of his license and his ship.

Aboard *San Salvador*, sailors were manning the winch and air pump. Whoever was on the bottom of the bay would have to return slowly to the surface if he was to do so safely. Claire knew that the pressure at sixty feet was roughly three atmospheres. Not so great as to guarantee bends for a diver who surfaced too rapidly, but certainly he would find himself in a risky zone.

She ducked her head beneath the surface and stroked down to a depth of ten feet or so. It was difficult to judge distances in this submarine world. A large fish approached her; she didn't know what species it was and hoped that it would not choose her for a snack. The fish swam up to within inches of her face, studied her curiously, then turned and swam away.

Whatever it was, it was certainly not a sardine.

She heard a steady throbbing. Something very large and dark was approaching. She realized, suddenly, that the sound came from the engines and propellers of a ship. If it struck her she didn't stand a chance. Swimming below the bay's surface as she was, she was invisible except to otters, sea lions, or fish — or possibly to other divers. She realized now that being invisible could be a danger.

She swam deeper. The sun's rays faded and the world grew dark. She unhooked the electric torch from her waistband and switched it on. Several more fish, their curiosity aroused by the beam of the torch, approached and inspected her, then lost interest and swam away.

Claire made her way cautiously. When she looked up and saw the dark shape of

San Salvador — at least, she thought it was *San Salvador* — she began her search for the diving cable.

The electric torch the Italians had provided was not very helpful. The bay water was murky and the torch's beam penetrated only a short distance.

She saw the lifeline and air hose just before colliding with them. She clung to the lifeline, a heavy woven hemp rope. She aimed the electric torch downward, using the lifeline as a guide. Both the hemp rope and the widening cone of illumination disappeared in the darkness of the bay.

Claire looked back toward the surface. She was too deep to see the sun or in fact to detect any illumination from above. For a panic-stricken moment she was unable to remember which direction was up and which was down, but after a little while she made a decision and began working her way along the lifeline. It was difficult going, holding the torch and pulling herself along, hand over hand, but she persisted.

She saw a peculiar, rounded shape not

far below her. She relinquished her grip on the rope and swam parallel to it, toward the curved surface. She estimated its cross-section at six or eight feet. As far as she could make out, its shape was that of a dome. She touched it and received the distinct impression that it was metallic.

She used her frog's feet to propel herself to the bay floor.

The metallic dome stood on four feet that held it above the silted bay bottom. There was enough clearance, Claire realized, to enter the bell-shaped chamber. Still, before making that move, she decided to circle the dome.

She directed the rays of her electric torch at the metallic wall. It appeared to be featureless. She pushed off from the bay floor and swam up about ten feet, using her frog's feet for power. Then she pointed the torch at the top of the dome. Although she had seen it from above, the murky bay water had prevented her from detecting the heavy metallic chain that hooked to its highest peak the way chains were attached to the much-publicized bathyscaphe that was in use for deep ocean exploration.

She swam back to the bay floor. She stood upright, pressing one hand against the wall of the dome for stability. A school of glistening silvery fish flashed by, reflecting the light of her torch. She studied the lower rim of the dome.

How could she have missed it? The air hose and lifeline that she had followed down to the dome — she had lost her awareness of them. It must be something about the pressure here sixty feet below the surface, or maybe something in the compressed air she was breathing. This was supposed to have been a brief familiarization dive. She had gone farther from shore and substantially deeper than the Italians had expected, and stayed under far longer. How much air had there been in her tank and how close was it to running out?

Would she have any warning? She could make an emergency ascent if necessary, she was fairly certain of that, but how great was her risk of the nitrogen-bubble disease, the bends?

She put those considerations out of her mind.

The air hose, the lifeline. She circled the dome until she found them. They entered the bell-shaped dome between two of its supporting feet and disappeared beneath the edge of the dome.

She flattened herself on her belly and maneuvered herself gingerly forward using her frog's feet for propulsion. Her air tank scraped on the lower edge of the dome as she passed beneath it.

She stood upright and shined her torch at a man wearing a full diving suit. When she directed her torch through the faceplate she recognized the patrician features of her employer and mentor, Akhenaton Beelzebub Chase.

He looked as astonished as she felt.

To her surprise she realized that the chamber was not filled with water. The opening at the bottom of the dome came halfway to her knees. Above that level the chamber was filled with air, but there was no visible source of replenishment. It was a good thing that she and Abel Chase both had air of their own, his coming from the pump on *San Salvador's* deck and hers from the tank strapped to her back.

Storage chests surrounded the interior of the chamber. Abel Chase pointed to one and led Claire Delacroix to it. He raised its heavy lid. Claire directed the beam of her electric torch into the chest. It was filled with exquisite blue-and-white porcelain bowls and cups. She reached into the chest and lifted one out. The porcelain was amazingly thin. She turned it over and found delicate images on the outside as well as the inside. Sharing the chest were figurines carved in green, yellow and red jade.

The Chinese residents of Monterey were right, then. There was a treasure lying on the bay's floor, and it was evidence of the legendary Chinese treasure fleet, not the Spanish galleon *Reina Ramona*.

With a metallic groan the chamber shifted, its heavy feet kicking up clouds of silt from the bay bottom. Claire Delacroix snatched a double handful of jade figurines from the storage chest. She stuffed them beneath her water-filled rubber suit.

She moved to open another chest. Abel Chase gestured as if to prevent her from doing so, but she got the lid open and looked inside. A pale face stared up at her. A man's body had been folded and stuffed into the chest. The body was garbed in warm, heavy clothing such as a diver might wear beneath his waterproof suit. Claire reached and saw a slit in the back of the man's heavy shirt. Blood had flowed and soaked the shirt.

She raised her eyes and locked glances with her employer. Within his rigid diving helmet he nodded. Claire was unable to discern the expression on his face, if indeed there was one.

The chamber shifted again. Claire Delacroix and Abel Chase ducked as the bell-shaped chamber lifted from the bay bottom and rose above them. Claire saw Chase tug at his lifeline. He reached and took her hand as he was lifted off the bottom and raised slowly, not vertically but diagonally toward the surface of Monterey Bay.

There was no way of telling how long the ascent took.

Neither Claire Delacroix nor Abel Chase wore a timepiece, nor were they able to converse. Claire's air supply had held out so far, but she was ready to separate herself from Chase and rise rapidly to the surface should that prove necessary, but in fact it did not.

First the water grew lighter and less murky, then the sun became visible, and then Claire Delacroix burst joyously into the fresh Pacific air.

Her happiness was short-lived.

She removed the breathing apparatus from her mouth and inhaled a great lung-full of fresh air. It was clear and bracing, tinctured with the scents and flavors of fecund brine. She swiveled her head, treading water with her frog's feet. She began to take inventory of her surroundings — there was *San Salvador*, crewmen working the air pump and winch, slowly hauling Abel Chase to the deck — when all Hades broke loose.

Another ship stood nearby, sailors

laboriously working over a power winch on her deck. Claire squinted through her goggles, then lifted them to get a better view. On the ship's hull was painted in faint, fading letters, *Maria Elena*. Johanna Cabrilho had mentioned *Maria Elena*, Captain Moretti's ship.

Rough hands grasped Claire's elbows. Black-hooded figures had risen from the water on her either side. Both wore goggles and breathers but she had no difficulty in recognizing the dangerously attractive Francesco DiMeo and the massive Rocco Cabrini.

Not uttering a word, the two Italians turned her in a coordinated maneuver. They started to propel her back toward their encampment at Lovers' Point, but they were confronted by the sight of Johanna Cabrilho's launch, racing toward them from the harbormaster's dockage. The launch was crowded with grim-looking men holding rifles and pistols at the ready. Claire identified Police Chief Mahoney among them. For the first time she recognized an expression of businesslike alertness on his features. Abel Chase's man-of-all-talents, Jenkins, sat beside Johanna Cabrilho in the launch's stern. He reached for Claire Delacroix and clasped her hand warmly, pulling her effortlessly into the boat.

Johanna Cabrilho throttled back the launch. Chief Mahoney lowered his Colt revolver and raised a megaphone to his mouth. He shouted at the two Italians, ordering them to return to shore. The Italians removed their mouthpieces and engaged in a rapid exchange in their own language. DiMeo offered Claire a gallant salute and they departed.

As soon as Claire was hauled into the launch she pointed to *Maria Elena* and blurted her experience to Johanna Cabrilho. Even as the harbormistress shot questions at her and Claire made her rapid-fire responses, the metallic dome broke water, dangling from its heavy chain.

'There is a dead man in there,' Claire Delacroix exclaimed. 'And I would bet that he's none other than the missing Mister Stimson.'

Johanna Cabrilho kicked the launch back to speed, heading toward *Maria Elena*. The sailors operating the winch on that ship released the ratchet and leaped to safety as the heavy chain ran out. The dome disappeared beneath the water. *Maria Elena* started to move, at first sluggishly, then with increasing speed.

Briefly the harbormistress's launch drew alongside the ship. Chief Mahoney shouted orders through his megaphone but to no avail. Instead, sailors appeared with rifles and began firing at the launch. Monterey police officers returned fire, but *Maria Elena* pulled away, heading for the open sea.

★   ★   ★

They assembled later in Abel Chase and Claire Delacroix's hotel suite. Only Jenkins was absent. Chief Mahoney reported that his men had arrested the three Italians on an open charge, but that he would probably have to release them — 'Unless you want to sign a complaint, Miss Delacroix.'

'On what grounds?'

'Why, attempted abduction. Maybe even assault.'

Food and hot coffee had been served again, and Chief Mahoney paused to tear off a generous gobbet of roast beef on rye and wash it down with a swig of coffee.

'On the other hand, them Eye-tally-ans claim that they'd loaned you one of their fancy new diving outfits for a little trial swim and you were tryin' to make off with it. They say they were just tryin' to get their equipment back.'

Claire said, 'I'd prefer if you just let them go, Chief.'

'Not so the *Maria Elena*,' Johanna Cabrilho put in. 'Captain Moretti and his henchmen will be up for everything from violating harbor regulations to piracy to — in all likelihood — the murder of the late Mister Stimson. The Coast Guard will round them up.'

Chief Mahoney swallowed and added his agreement. 'And thanks to you, Dr. Chase, for sending your man Jenkins to track the *Maria Elena* in that whirlybird thingumbob of yours. They won't get away now. They don't stand a chance.'

Abel Chase nodded and smiled acknowledgment of Mahoney's gratitude. 'We might mount another attempt to recover the iron chamber and the treasure. I do consider locating that one of our more noteworthy achievements.'

'Yes indeedy,' Chief Mahoney agreed. 'And we'll need that *corpus delicti*, that's for certain.'

'Possibly,' Johanna Cabrilho responded. 'But *Maria Elena* was already moving when she dropped the dome. I'm afraid it fell right into the trench. If that happened we'll never get down to it. It's gone forever.'

'Even so,' Claire Delacroix added, 'we do have something to show for our adventure.' Without another word she walked to her own room, returning with the magnificent jades she had removed from the treasure chest in the dome.

She set them carefully on a polished tabletop as if placing them for a museum display. 'These should settle some disputes among historians and curators, I think.'

'Indeed,' Abel Chase agreed. 'I shall have to prepare myself for the adulation of the academic world.'

5

The Case Of The Bilious Bookman

Clad in bias-cut jacket, woolen skirt, and comfortable shoes, Claire Delacroix sat facing the tall windows that offered so breathtaking a view of the town of Berkeley below the *faux* Tudor mansion, the waters of San Francisco Bay, the City of San Francisco and the rural Marin headlands across the Golden Gate. Crews of workers labored mightily constructing two great bridges. One would cross the Bay and would permit rail and automotive travel between the city and the East Bay. The other would span the Golden Gate itself.

While the lissome blonde Claire Delacroix mused on the scene before her she played an Arpa Doppia harp built some four hundred years earlier in Milan. Incongruously, the melodies that she plucked from the harp's three rows of strings were a medley of tunes by the American composer Irving Berlin. Seated nearby at a massive desk, silver-filigreed Waterman in hand, Akhenaton Beelzebub Chase composed a sympathetic letter. In flawless German, Chase wrote:

My Dear Herr Czinner:
   Our mutual friend, Mr. Douglas Fairbanks, Jr., has informed me of the disgraceful manner in which Herr Goebbels has maligned you and Frau Bergner-Czinner and sabotaged the premiere of your film, Catherine the Great. The increasingly violent and dictatorial conduct of the National Socialist regime in Germany have given pause to thoughtful and civilized persons throughout the world.
   It is my understanding that you have left Germany, a wise move, which of course many of your co-religionists and numerous other decent persons have chosen to follow. The psychopathology of the current regime in Berlin may appeal to revanchists and the neurotic impulses of —

At this point both the softly cheering notes of the Arpa Doppia and the nearly inaudible scratching of the Waterman were interrupted by the arrival of Leicester Jenkins, Chase's major domo and man of all work. Jenkins was clad in butler's livery. He carried with him a black instrument, its electrical wire wound carefully around its long neck.

'A telephone call for Miss Delacroix. A Mr. van Hopkins, Miss.'

Claire Delacroix shot a questioning glance at Abel Chase. There was no need to put into words her query.

'You may take the call in here, Delacroix.'

Claire Delacroix nodded to Jenkins, who plugged the telephone into a specially installed receptacle, then departed. While she spoke, Abel Chase stood first at the window, watching the Bay and the traffic that moved endlessly on its surface. After a few moments he turned and left the room, depressed, perhaps, by the topic he had been addressing in his letter to Czinner.

Upon completing her telephone conversation Claire Delacroix also left the room. She found her employer in the mansion's great kitchen. He had seated himself at the table there and sipped from a cup of coffee brewed from Puerto Rican mountain-grown beans. He rose, flushed, and offered Claire Delacroix a cup of the beverage.

She accepted.

'I fear that conditions are going to get worse before they get better,' Chase said. 'You have heard, I suppose, of the Nazis' tactic of intimidating audiences and preventing the exhibition of Paul Czinner's film. They've taken *Il Duce's* totalitarian regime in Italy as their model, and if anything they are doing the Italians one better. Or worse. And yet Mussolini claims to be a violinist and Hitler a painter. How odd that two self-proclaimed artistic souls should become such brutal dictators.'

He shook his head sadly, then managed a smile. 'I trust your telephone conversation was of a more pleasant nature. I would not wish to pry, of course.'

'Nothing very private,' Claire Delacroix replied. 'It was Burt van Hopkins.'

Abel Chase frowned. 'That writer for the San Francisco *Call*?'

'The very one.'

'I did not know you were acquainted.'

'I met him when we were students at the University of California. We've kept in touch. We share certain interests. Rare books and manuscripts, for one.'

'Ah.' Chase's comment was noncommittal.

'He's been covering a story that he thought would interest me, and in fact it does.' She smiled. 'It wouldn't surprise me if you received a call from your friend Captain Baxter about it.'

'A homicide, then.' Chase lowered his cup. It was the plain but colorful fiesta ware used in the kitchen, rather than the delicate Spode that he and Claire Delacroix dined upon at mealtimes. 'Now there is something we can deal with. The problems of the world are of such a scale, I am almost ready to accept the theories of inevitability that one finds in the works of Spengler and Marx. But sometimes, at least, a murder can be addressed and a culprit can be brought to the bar of justice.'

He was in the very midst of carrying his now empty cup and saucer to the sink when the telephone bell could be heard once more.

Jenkins appeared in the doorway.

'Sorry to interrupt again, sir. It's Captain Baxter.'

Abel Chase and Claire Delacroix exchanged knowing glances. To Jenkins, Chase said, 'Fine, I'll take the call.'

Within the hour Chase and Delacroix had bundled into warm clothing and were standing beneath the *port cochère*. Claire Delacroix had added a thick outer coat and heavy leather purse to her outfit. Leicester Jenkins, attired now in somber chauffeur's costume, brought the Hispano Suiza from the former carriage house, now adapted as garage and mechanic's bay, and leaped out to assist his master and Claire Delacroix into the rear seat. He spread a lap robe over them, then climbed behind the steering wheel and set the car in motion.

As soon as they arrived at the bayside dock, Abel Chase and Claire Delacroix transferred from automobile to ferry. Jenkins pulled away in the Hispano Suiza. Chase and Delacroix turned their faces toward San Francisco. Standing at the rail, they breathed the crisp, salt-tinged air.

'Shall I go first, Dr. Chase?' Delacroix asked. 'I'll give you the information Burt van Hopkins gave me. We'll see if it matches Cleland Baxter's news.'

Abel Chase having given his consent, Claire Delacroix began.

'You know there are a number of expert bookmen in San Francisco. And of course you know that the peculiar trade in which they engage seems to attract eccentrics of every stripe.'

Chase grunted.

'By far the most noteworthy bookman I ever met, and by reputation the most notorious, is Happy Henry Previtali.' Claire Delacroix grinned at the memory.

'Enrico Vittorio Previtali, to give him his full name. He specialized in musical first editions and incunabula. His shop on Post Street is famous throughout the book world. Scouts have even come from

Book Row in New York to examine his stock. And of course he published important catalogues for decades. One of a dying breed. Grey hair that he never combed, a three-day beard that he managed to keep at just that length. Suspicious, angry, a legend. That's why they called him Hap. It was short for Happy Henry. Burt van Hopkins told me that the other scouts were afraid to go out with Previtali. He could go through a collection and find everything of value, quick as a whistle. And it didn't matter if the other scouts got there first. Previtali would go through their leavings and come up with a rare Poe or Hawthorne or Mark Twain and buy it for a song.'

'A fabulous character.' Abel Chase offered a special smile, the kind that Claire Delacroix saw on his face only when a new case was offered to him, one that he felt worthy of his mettle.

'But you spoke of him in the past tense. Why is that?'

'Burt van Hopkins told me that Enrico Previtali is dead.'

'Of natural causes?'

'No.'

'I thought not,' Abel Chase said. His face was neutral but his voice sounded almost jolly.

Claire Delacroix raised her eyes to the tall structures of downtown San Francisco and to the clock tower that rose above the Ferry Building. 'What is the plan, Dr. Chase?'

'Clel Baxter is sending a car to meet us at the pier. I would be pleased to have your company and assistance, Delacroix, unless you have some other preference.'

'Actually, I do. Burt van Hopkins will be at the Ferry Building, also. If you don't mind, I'll accompany him. He's covering the story from the viewpoint of the book-collecting world.'

'That might be useful. Very well. If you wish to communicate with me, telephone the house and leave a message with Jenkins. I will do the same.'

The ferry pulled into its slip and Abel Chase and Claire Delacroix disembarked.

Captain Cleland Baxter of the homicide squad, San Francisco Police Department, rushed forward to shake hands with Abel

Chase. 'Major Chase, sir. Corporal Baxter reporting!' he grinned. He was natty in his blue uniform with its polished buttons and gold badge.

Abel Chase returned the greeting. 'That was long ago, Cleland. You're the captain now, and I'm just a friend.'

Baxter turned to Claire Delacroix. 'You're looking lovely as ever, Miss. Along to watch the master at work?'

Claire Delacroix kept a straight face by chewing the inside of her cheek. When she could speak she said, 'No, Captain. As a matter of fact — oh, there he is now!'

A ruddy-faced, stocky man in tweeds with matching cap was climbing from a Nash coupé drawn to the curb outside the Ferry Building. He ran from the coupé to the trio. He grasped Claire Delacroix's hands in his own. His hands were muscular and callused; hers, graceful and smooth. A look passed between them and he drew back.

'Captain Baxter, good to see you.' He shook hands with the police official. 'And you, sir, must be the famous Dr. Chase.'

He extended his hand. 'Burt van Hopkins, San Francisco *Call*.'

'I've read your stories,' Chase said.

'Well, must be going.' Van Hopkins took Claire Delacroix's hand once more and the two of them ran to his Nash. Claire Delacroix opened her door for herself and the car zipped away into the traffic on the Embarcadero.

Abel Chase and Cleland Baxter stood looking after the coupé.

'Ain't it wonderful,' Baxter exclaimed. 'Ain't it just wonderful to behold.'

Abel Chase said, 'There must be something unusual about this case for you to ask me to assist you, Baxter. Perhaps your office would be a good place to discuss it.'

'As you wish, sir.' Baxter ushered Abel Chase into the police cruiser that stood at the ready. 'Headquarters, Mulrooney.'

They made small talk as the policeman drove them to the downtown headquarters building. Baxter had heard of Abel Chase's aerial adventure in the case involving the disappearance of one Karol Raynor from an experimental aeroplane two miles above San Francisco Bay. It was a pleasure to see Dr. Chase fully recovered from his injuries. And Abel Chase was equally pleased to hear that Cleland Baxter's wife and house full of daughters were all in good spirits and blossoming health.

Once settled in Baxter's office the one-time comrades set to work, a carafe of coffee at the police official's elbow and a folder of reports spread on Baxter's desk.

'Look at this, Abel.'

Baxter, as was his custom, had lapsed into the familiar form of address once they were past their initial exchanges. 'You see, here are all the reports, from the moment the call came in from the beat officer right up to the coroner's analysis. It's a nasty case, and a puzzler, I'll say.'

Abel Chase lifted a police form, studied it, then dropped it and picked up another. He took his time, reaching occasionally for a sip of coffee. An ormolu clock stood on a shelf near Baxter's deck, ticking steadily. Finally Chase looked up.

'Fascinating. I see there is only one

autopsy report but two laboratory reports. Why is that, Baxter?'

'Well, you know, sir, diners do keel over at restaurant tables. Sometimes they've had a bit too much vino. The management sees that they get home safely and they sleep it off and nothing is made of it. But what if the customer has a heart attack? A rarity, sir, but it happens. Management gets very upset. Bad for business. But this time two diners passed out. Very odd. Very odd. The owner tried to revive them and one of them came around. The other didn't, so the owner called an ambulance. One fellow was quite all right. It must have been the excitement of his companion's collapse that got him. He plain out fainted. But the other fellow died before they ever got to the hospital.'

'Very good.' Abel Chase stroked his chin with forefinger and thumb. He shaved closely each day, his face smooth save for a meticulously trimmed, pencil-thin moustache. Even so, his beard, had he chosen to grow one, would have been heavy and dark. Consequently, his jaw suggested a dark blue. 'And I see from the coroner's report that the victim died of acute strychnine poisoning.' He raised his eyes to meet those of Cleland Baxter. 'How was the poison administered?'

'Everything the men had on their table went to the lab, sir. Of course the chemist suspected that the strychnine had been put in the wine that they shared. It was a bottle of Valpolicella imported from Italy.'

'Yes?'

'No, sir. The wine was fine. Wasn't in the marinara sauce, either, or in the piccata sauce on their veal.'

'A pretty puzzle,' Chase commented. 'It must have been — ' He jerked a thumb at the coffee carafe near Cleland Baxter's elbow.

'No.' Baxter sprang to his feet, a man packed with energy that could not long remain still. 'It was in the cannoli.'

'Oh, oh, very pretty, Clel. I imagine the cannoli was chilled. I cannot imagine any decent Italian serving it any other way. The shock of the icy dessert would certainly distract the victim long enough for the strychnine to enter his system. It's a very quick-acting toxin. The victim would be unconscious before he had realized what was happening to him, and death would occur within minutes.'

'That's what the coroner and the lab concluded.' Baxter was pacing impatiently.

'And the laboratory report indicates' — Abel Chase paused meditatively — 'that the victim's unconsumed cannoli contained strychnine while his companion's had none. Which leads one to wonder, Was the strychnine intended for a specific victim, or was it placed at random?'

Without waiting for Baxter to respond, Chase suggested, 'Perhaps we should visit the scene of the death.'

Without another word both men reached for their hats — Baxter's, a police captain's rather gaudy headpiece; Chase's, a dark fedora that harmonized with his topcoat and suit.

It was a short ride via police cruiser to North Beach, the city's center of Italian immigrant life. At Captain Baxter's instructions the driver pulled to the curb in front of Tommasino's Palermo Café. The restaurant was open but the hour was a quiet one between the rush of noontime and the arrival of the dinner crowd. Further, word had spread of the death the night before and customers were understandably reluctant to patronize the establishment that had been the scene of the poisoning.

Giampiero Tommasino was a rotund Italian clad incongruously in tuxedo jacket and white chef's apron. He met Baxter and Chase at the entrance to his establishment and ushered them inside. 'Captain,' he said, 'where would you like to sit? You want a table? You want some food? Some vino? Anything for you, for your friend.' He made a quarter-bow to Abel Chase.

'Dr. Chase is a professor at the University of California,' Baxter told the restaurateur. 'Seat us where the unfortunate duo sat last night, if you please. And bring a chair for yourself. We need to talk.'

Tommasino showed them to a corner table. It was situated near a plate glass window that offered a view of the street scene outside. 'You see,' Tommasino said,

'Signor Previtali is a regular customer, was a regular customer here. We always give him good treatment. We make everybody happy, you know, this is a very competitive business.'

He pronounced the words carefully and with emphasis. *Competitive. Business.*

'But you take good care of your regulars,' he continued, 'they take good care of you.'

'Yes, yes. Get on with it, Tommasino.'

'Of course, I am so sorry.' A waiter passed nearby and the restaurateur waved him over. The waiter bowed. He wore a white shirt, black bow tie and black trousers, and a short apron. Tommasino said, 'Please, Captain. Doctor. Have something. Maybe a bottle of fine vino. Maybe some tiramisu with an espresso.'

Abel Chase said, 'Perhaps just the espresso, Mr. Tommasino.'

The restaurateur motioned to the waiter, who disappeared.

'Signor Previtali, he was one of my oldest customers, one of my best customers. A difficult man, sometimes, but a great scholar. He knew every opera ever written, every great singer, everything.'

'Who was his companion?' Chase queried.

'Him I didn't know,' the restaurateur admitted. '*Signor* Previtali usually dined alone. Sometimes I would sit at his table, he would invite me to sit down. He used to talk about finding books, buying, selling books. And he would talk about music. At night, you know, we have music here. A violinist and a singer. Sometimes *Signor* Previtali, he would correct the singers. They got very upset. But *Signor* Previtali, he insisted. *Sing it right*, he would say, *sing it right*.'

'That's all right,' Cleland Baxter interjected. 'Previtali's companion wound up at the General Hospital. We have his name and address. He gave us a statement, it's being typed up now. That's why you didn't see it in the file, Major.'

Chase acknowledged the information with a nod. Then he asked the rotund Tommasino, 'What happened last night?' Chase looked up. The waiter had returned with a tray bearing a steaming pot, three cups, a platter of biscotti. Tommasino nodded and the waiter departed. Chase dipped a biscotto in his espresso and brought the pastry to his mouth.

'Last night the music was all Puccini,' Tommasino enthused. 'All the divine Puccini. *La Rondine. Trittico. La Fanciulla del West*. For one time *Signor* Previtali made no corrections. He was in very happy mood. He applauded my singer. His friend was more quiet. They finish their meal, all except for dessert. The waiter brings them cannoli. I looked at their bill after. I got no money for their meal. I got to know how much I lose. I looked at their bill. No cannoli on it.'

Abel Chase pursed his lips. 'That is very strange. Is their waiter here today?' Tommasino shook his head so hard that a bead of perspiration flew from his brow. It landed and soaked into the white table cloth. 'He didn't show up today. I phone his house, no answer.'

Cleland Baxter asked, 'What was his name.'

'Giordano. Alcide Giordano.'

'Where did he live?'

Tommasino gave an address not far from the restaurant.

'How long had be been working here?'

'Not so long. He wasn't so good a waiter anyhow, I was thinking of letting him go. But you know, jobs are hard to find now, I was sorry for him, I didn't want to let him go if I could help it. But now he's gone. Even if he shows up again, he's gone, that Giordano.'

'Did anyone else have cannoli last night?'

'We sell seven cannoli desserts.'

'No other problems.'

'None.'

Baxter turned to Abel Chase. 'What do you think?'

'We need a look at brother Giordano's digs.'

They left the restaurant and proceeded to the address Tommasino had given them. It was only a few blocks away in hilly, noisy North Beach.

The building was a rundown Victorian, long since divided into rental units. There was no answer when they knocked on Giordano's door but they heard a cat crying inside the apartment. Baxter summoned the driver of the police cruiser that had brought them to North Beach and after a brief exchange the officer produced a set of miniature tools. It took less than a minute to unlock the door.

As they opened the door an angry ginger cat sped past them and disappeared down the wooden steps to the sidewalk. Cleland Baxter entered the apartment, followed by Abel Chase. The driver remained outside.

'Looks like our boy left in a hurry,' Baxter said.

The bed was crudely made but dresser drawers hung open, half emptied. The closet door was open and a few gaps were visible in the clothing hung on a warped wooden rod and the row of scuffed shoes on the floor.

It was a small apartment, little more than a furnished room. A window looked out on passing traffic. In one corner a sink dripped steadily. The orange stain on the chipped, yellowed porcelain sink testified that the dripping had been going on for some time. Every sign indicated that Giordano had packed hastily and departed in a hurry.

'What do you think, Clel?'

'I think this fellow knew what he was doing at the restaurant. He must have been paid to administer that poison, and once he'd earned his dirty money he knew that he wasn't safe. Either we'd get him or his employers would. So he skedaddled out of town.'

Abel Chase nodded. 'I think you're right.' He walked to the room's sole window and looked into the street. 'If he has a car he's probably in Mexico by now, ready to find a hole and hide in it. If he doesn't have a car he's on a train right now. Or maybe hitchhiking out of the state. Baxter, you ought to check on that. See if there's an auto registered to him. I don't think there's much chance you'll catch him and it probably doesn't matter very much if you do. He's the killer, in the sense that he served the fatal portion of cannoli to the victim. But it's most unlikely that he was acting on his own. Somebody put him up to it. That's who interests me.'

Baxter was wandering around the furnished room. He pulled open a previously closed dresser drawer, rummaged through its contents, and slid it shut. He repeated the operation until he reached the bottom drawer, then stood up triumphantly, a pair of round objects in one hand. He had used a pair of grey undershorts to hold them.

'Have a look at this, Major!'

Clearly, Baxter's discovery had shocked him back into a degree of formality.

Abel Chase stood beside the police captain. As if by plan, a ray of bright sunlight pierced the window and glittered off Baxter's double prize. 'Brother Giordano must have used this hypodermic syringe to get the strychnine into the cannoli. And look at the bottle — it's still half full.'

'Or half empty,' Abel Chase grinned.

'These will go to the lab, of course.' Baxter slipped the syringe and the bottle, carefully wrapped in Alcide Giordano's underpants, into the side pocket of his heavy uniform coat.

They headed for the door. Moments

later Captain Baxter handed the underwear-wrapped implements to his driver, Officer Mulrooney. 'Take good care of these. And be careful, don't stick yourself with that needle. You're a married man, aren't you, Mulrooney? The department can't afford another widow's pension.'

Climbing into the backseat of the police cruiser, Abel Chase said, 'We have this much, Cleland. We know who Mr. Previtali's companion was. The criminals might have been smarter to have Giordano administer strychnine in both desserts. Our good fortune as well as that of Mr. Stuart Thielemann.'

The visor of his police official's cap shading his eyes from the late afternoon sun, Captain Baxter smiled at Abel Chase. 'You've an amazing memory, Abel. I've always known that. You never forget a detail.'

'Thank you.'

'And since Tommasino didn't know the name of the victim's companion, how do you know it?'

'He was Stuart Thielemann. He carried a business card. It was in the case file on your own desk, Cleland. Surely you saw it. Even if Thielemann's statement wasn't there yet, the card was all one needed.'

'Ah, Abel, that's why you were a battalion commander and I was just a corporal in the war. Well, and what information did you glean from the card — beside Thielemann's name, that is.'

Chase smiled. At last Baxter had lapsed into the informality of calling him Abel. 'It identified Mr. Thielemann as an expert appraiser of and consultant on rare books and manuscripts. A polite term for what people in the trade call a book scout — or so Miss Delacroix tells me. It gave his telephone number and an address which might be either that of his office or his home. In the Monadnock Building on Market Street.'

'Well then, shall we head back to my office and see if Thielemann's statement is ready, Abel?'

Chase considered briefly, then shook his head. 'I think not yet. Let's pay a visit to Mr. Thielemann.'

Baxter's driver ferried them to San

Francisco's main thoroughfare and dropped them off at the Monadnock Building. Inside, a directory listed *Stuart Thielemann, Fine Books and Manuscripts*, along with an office number on an upper story. Chase and Baxter rode up in an elevator operated by a septuagenarian in pseudo-military garb.

Stuart Thielemann, Fine Books and Manuscripts — by appointment only was lettered on the pebbled glass of a dark-stained door. The lettering was not of recent vintage, as shown by its faded and chipped appearance. Baxter rapped with his knuckles. There was no response. He rapped again, more loudly.

A hoarse voice called out, 'Can't you read?'

Baxter growled. 'San Francisco Police Department, Thielemann. Open up!'

'I don't know anything. I told you everything last night. Go away.'

'Open the door or I'll knock it down and take you in, Thielemann.'

Someone, presumably Stuart Thielemann, muttered and shuffled inside the office.

Footsteps padded to the door. The occupant pulled it back a few inches and Cleland Baxter shoved it open, striding into the room.

Abel Chase followed him and shut the door.

A disheveled figure backed away from the two newcomers. He looked them up and down, clearly relieved at the sight of Baxter's uniform and badge.

★   ★   ★

Claire Delacroix sat beside Burt van Hopkins as the reporter slipped his little Nash coupé into a parking space in front of the storefront on Post Street. Before he had time even to shut off the motor the slim woman had planted her feet on the cement pavement and was studying the exterior of the establishment.

The building was of sturdy stone facing. A show window bore the name of the business, *Enrico Previtali, Rare Books and Manuscripts*. Below this were listed days and hours of trade. A seal had been placed on the front door and a uniformed patrolman stood before it, feet spread, hands clasped behind his back.

Burt van Hopkins walked up to the patrolman and smiled. 'How're you doing, Oliver?'

The patrolman grinned. 'Still celebrating, Burt. Any time you want to bet on a boxing match, I'm your man.'

'I guess I should stick to the book beat, Ollie. Oh, this is Miss Delacroix.'

The patrolman tipped his hat, 'Pleased to meet you, Miss.'

Claire responded politely.

Officer Oliver said, 'Mr. van Hopkins here, he sure can pick 'em. Fighters, I mean. That frog-eating Maurice Dubois went up against Panama Al Brown. Do you follow the fights, Miss?'

'Not very much.'

The officer adopted a boxer's pose. 'I've been following Brown since he broke in. A classy bantamweight. He's the champ. Getting a little bit old now, but he still has the stuff, Miss. He not only took Dubois down, he kayoed him in two. In two, would you believe it? And Mr. van Hopkins and me had a little wager on the bout. I'm still celebrating. Any time you want to get down another wager, Burt, look me up.'

Van Hopkins said, 'We need to look around the store, Ollie.'

'No can do,' Oliver told him. 'Owner was murdered last night. Store's sealed. Might be vital evidence inside.'

After a moment he said, 'Golly, it's cold out here. Watch the store for me, would you, Burt? I'm headed down to the diner there at the corner for a cup of coffee. I'll be right back, except they're awfully slow sometimes. You get me? They're awfully slow sometimes.'

As Oliver strolled away Claire Delacroix remarked, 'At least he didn't wink.'

'He's a good fellow. Let's get to work.'

Van Hopkins pulled a massive collection of keys from his jacket pocket and set to work on the door. Claire Delacroix stood facing away from the door, blocking van Hopkins from the sight of casual pedestrians. She could see the diner where Oliver had headed. It was on the other side of Post Street, and the blue-clad policeman entered, hung his uniform cap on a hook and seated himself with his back to the street with every appearance of being in no hurry at all.

The inside of Previtali's shop had the unmistakable smell of old books. Claire Delacroix's nostrils flared and an involuntary smile crossed her face. Burt van Hopkins walked behind the counter and reached down. Electric lights flared. Clearly, van Hopkins knew the place well. Claire Delacroix had passed it on occasion, on her few visits to San Francisco, but she soon decided that the stock of this store would be beyond her budget and passed it by.

The room was lined from floor to ceiling with bookshelves. The shelves were packed and piles of unshelved books stood on the floor. A rolling ladder gave access to the higher shelves. A glass display case ran from the end of the counter, just enough space between it and the wall behind it to permit access to the bottom rows of books.

'I'm sorry that old Happy Henry bought the farm,' van Hopkins said. He gestured with an outstretched hand.

'Look at this place. There's a back room, too, and another room full of books upstairs.'

Claire Delacroix leaned over the display case, studying its contents. She asked van Hopkins what he thought of Previtali.

'He was the nastiest bozo in the book racket, and the smartest. He was totally paranoid and hated his customers. Unless he knew you he was always afraid you were a scout, and he wouldn't let anybody see his stock for fear they'd find a treasure and buy it for a song and sell it for a bundle. Of course he used to do exactly that himself when he was younger. Still liked to go out and scout right to the end, and when he slipped a sleeper out from under a competitor's nose he'd invite his victim out for dinner and gloat. His favorite place was Tommasino's up in North Beach. Not a cheap joint. But he did well. Kept up this store, had a nice apartment, drove a new Auburn. Depression didn't seem to hurt him.'

'But why would somebody kill him? Who would do it? A rival? Somebody who felt he'd gypped them?'

Van Hopkins stood beside Claire Delacroix. For some reason they both lowered their eyes. Perhaps it was the appeal of the treasures in the display case.

'I don't know,' van Hopkins said. 'I was just getting interested in Previtali. I've known him for years, as long as I've been on the book beat for the *Call*, but he kept me at arm's length. He used to let me in the store but he watched me like a hawk. You have to keep your ear to the rail in the newspaper business and I was hearing odd things about him.'

From outside the store there was a screech of brakes and the sound of two autos colliding. Claire Delacroix ran to the front window and studied the scene. When she turned back to face Burt van Hopkins she smiled. 'Nobody hurt, but a couple of fellows are going at it over who was at fault.'

Van Hopkins nodded. 'Good. That will keep Oliver busy when he finishes his coffee.'

Claire Delacroix returned to the glass display case. She peered behind it, walked to the end and returned. She perched on a tall stool behind the cash register.

'Odd things.'

Van Hopkins said, 'Eh?'

'You said you heard odd things about Enrico Previtali. What odd things?'

'Oh.' Van Hopkins seemed flustered. He moved to the end of the display case closest to the cash register and looked at Claire Delacroix. 'He was selling some remarkable items.'

'First editions?'

Van Hopkins shook his head. 'Musical manuscripts. Holograph copies of important works, some of them early sketches. You can't imagine.'

'Try me.'

'The scouts were buzzing. I got this from Stuart Thielemann. Another legendary scout, but not like Enrico Previtali. Happy Henry was a great scout and a smart businessman. Poor Stuart was a great scout but a lousy businessman. I should say, is. Too fond of John Barleycorn, too fond of fast women, too fond of poker games. He comes up with real finds and has to make a quick sale to keep from having a nasty accident and winding up in the hospital.'

He paused for a breath. The sound of the argument rose from Post Street. Surely Oliver must be there by now, trying to calm things down until the tow trucks arrived.

'Thielemann finally told me what Previtali was selling. Holograph copies of important compositions. He sold a preliminary sketch for Brahms' *Serenade in D*. He sold a Talus holograph. It was only part of one page of *derilinquat impius* but can you imagine? The Brahms was nineteenth century, that was precious enough, but the Talus — a piece of sacred music written almost four hundred years ago, and here it is in the composer's own hand? It was unbelievable.'

'Where did he get them?'

Van Hopkins shrugged. 'That's what I was trying to find out. Previtali wouldn't talk to me about it. Last time I came in here and tried to get some information he threw me out of his store, threatened to — '

'Call the coppers and have you arrested?'

Van Hopkins shook his head. ' — shoot me. And I think he meant it. There's a gun back there where you are, Claire. He was always afraid of being robbed and he kept it loaded and ready to use. I'll bet a sawbuck it's still in the drawer under the register.'

Claire Delacroix set her heavy purse on the floor and pulled open a drawer, shut it, opened another and nodded.

'You win, Burt.'

She stood up holding the weapon.

'Enrico was an antiquarian, all right. He's got an 1872 Adams five-shot. Kept it oiled and loaded, too. He wasn't kidding around.' She disappeared behind the counter, then reappeared, heavy purse clutched in her hands.

'Previtali wouldn't talk,' van Hopkins said, 'and Thielemann insisted he didn't know where Previtali was getting these unbelievable treasures. But he told me one more thing that I absolutely couldn't believe.'

He leaned back, smugly waiting for

Claire Delacroix to take the bait. She didn't disappoint him.

'What was that?'

Van Hopkins leaned halfway across the counter; Claire Delacroix leaned forward, balancing on the tall stool. She almost tipped over and had to grab van Hopkins' sleeve to steady herself. The weave of his jacket was rough. Even after she moved her hand from his sleeve to the glass display case her palm tingled.

'Thielemann says that Previtali had a holograph copy of *Vivat Bacchus*.'

'No!' Claire looked into van Hopkins' eyes and was not sure whether he thought she was mocking him.

Apparently he decided she was not. 'Yes, Pedrillo and Osman's duet. A wonderful moment in *Die Entführung dem Serail*. Sublime! And in Mozart's own hand! It's like finding a Shakespeare manuscript. It's unbelievable.'

'Did he sell it?'

'No.'

'Where is it? What will become of it now?'

Van Hopkins shrugged. 'I don't know if

there are any heirs. I'm pretty sure that Previtali was a bachelor.'

'No surprise there.'

'The court will probably take control of the estate, sell everything, pay itself as much as it can get away with, and hold the rest in escrow.'

'And the Mozart?'

'If they find it, it will bring a fortune. Can you imagine the competition — every museum worth its salt, universities, private collectors. Probably Hitler will want it back for some *Reichsmuseum*. Huh? And *Il Duce* will have a fit, he claims to be such a music-lover.'

Van Hopkins paused. 'But first they have to find it.'

Someone was rapping at the show window. Claire Delacroix and Burt van Hopkins looked up. How long had they been in the store, captured by the spell of old books . . . and perhaps by each other? The sky outside was darkening and streetlamps had begun to glow through an early evening mist.

Officer Oliver was waving at them, his lips moving with inaudible words. Behind him the evidence of the earlier collision had disappeared and automobiles moved briskly along Post Street.

Claire Delacroix followed Burt van Hopkins to the front door and out into Post Street. His Nash coupé stood invitingly at the curb. Once inside the car van Hopkins raised his wristwatch to catch the light of passing cars. 'It's getting late, Claire. Half-past six. What are your plans?'

'Actually, I'm pretty hungry.'

Van Hopkins volunteered that he had a favorite Northern Chinese restaurant out on Geary. If Claire was interested . . .

At the restaurant she dropped a coin in a pay telephone and gave the operator the number of the Chase mansion in Berkeley. She chatted briefly with Leicester Jenkins, then returned to the table. She and van Hopkins shared a dinner of searing Hunan pepper beef and ice cold beer. They spoke of books and of bookmen, and inevitably reverted to Enrico Previtali.

'You never told me who was buying those amazing treasures that Mr. Previtali was selling, Burt.'

'Ahah!' He grinned. 'That's part of the mystery. I couldn't get anything at all out of Previtali himself, and his scout Thielemann closed up as tight as a clam when I tried to find out where the manuscripts were coming from. But he did let slip where they were going. There are only three people in this town with the taste and the budget to collect that kind of treasure. Plus, of course, the museums and universities. But apparently Previtali was selling privately. There might be some question about the provenance of the manuscripts, and he didn't want to get dragged into a court case.'

The meal was drawing to a close and Claire Delacroix alternated a sip of hot jasmine tea with one of cold amber beer. 'Okay, Burt, do I have to drag it out of you? Who are the big three?'

'Well, one of them is — was — Previtali himself. Of course he's out of the picture for two reasons.'

'One,' Claire Delacroix supplied, 'he's the seller, he'd hardly be the buyer. Two, he's dead.'

'Right.'

Their waiter laid a small tray on their table. On it were their tab and two fortune cookies.

Van Hopkins looked at the check, pulled his wallet from his pocket and dropped a banknote on the tray.

Claire nodded toward the tray. 'Thanks. I'll get the next one. And who are the other two collectors?'

'A fellow named Bernie Zapf and the widder lady Loretta Hamilton Hodge.'

Claire Delacroix pursed her lips and emitted a low whistle. 'Laura Hodge. She has more money than Amadeo Giannini and Cornelius Vanderbilt put together. She owns half of Nob Hill and would buy the rest but nobody else wants to sell. But she seldom goes there anyhow. She goes to the opera opening every year, I've seen her there. Everyone says she lives like a hermit in her mansion in St. Francis Woods the rest of the year.'

'I think you exaggerate a little, but you're not far off.'

'And who's Barnie Zipf?'

'Bernie Zapf.'

'All right. Who is he?'

'He's a novelist.'

'Never heard of him.'

'Uses a pseudonym. And what that is, is the best kept secret since the first draft of the Versailles Treaty. But scuttlebutt in the book trade says that he's been incredibly successful. Yet he lives in a modest house on Valencia Street, drives a little four-cylinder Whippet car, wears a shiny suit. But he's a legendary collector. He's another character. A real ruffian, supposed to come out of the Tenderloin. Story is he killed two or three men in the old days, back in Mayor Rolph's first term. He was a private detective for a few years, and not a very ethical one. He's still connected with the Black Hand, and he writes murder mysteries. At least that's the word. Figure it out if you can.'

The waiter was approaching again. Van Hopkins snatched the two fortune cookies off the little tray and waved the waiter away.

'Nobody's talking officially, but according to Stuart Thielemann, Zapf got the

Brahms and Loretta Hamilton Hodge got the Talus.'

'And the Mozart? Where does that fit into the picture?'

'Hodge and Zapf would both do anything to get their hands on it. But Previtali wouldn't sell. Anything else in his shop, even items out of his personal collection, but not the Mozart. In fact, he denied that there was such an article, but nobody believed him.'

Claire Delacroix looked up. She and Burt van Hopkins were the only customers left in the restaurant. She said, 'I think they want to close up and go home.'

'We haven't read our fortunes yet.'

'We can take them with us.'

Van Hopkins reddened. 'Aren't you afraid of missing the last ferry back to the East Bay?'

Claire Delacroix said, 'No.'

First thing the next morning, Burt van Hopkins telephoned his editor. He'd filed enough extra copy in the past week to keep the Book Beat column going for a while. The conversation was brief and van Hopkins grunted with satisfaction as he dropped the earpiece back onto its hook.

Claire Delacroix had started a pot of coffee going and poured orange juice for them. 'We either have to wrap this up today or I'm going out and buy some new duds.'

Van Hopkins grinned. 'I have a friend at the City of Paris. You'll get something nice.'

'I want to talk to Barney Zip.'

'Bernie Zapf.'

'And Loretta Hodge.'

'Zapf should be easier. I know him.'

'Think we should phone for an appointment?'

'That's the last thing we should do. Zapf has a well-trained wife. She'd say he's out of town, she doesn't know when he'll be back, there's no way to get a message to him, and go take a long walk on a short pier while you're at it.'

'Well then — what do we do?'

'He's got a few favorite hang-outs, some near his house and a couple in the Tenderloin. Chances are he'll be at one of them.'

'When does he write his books?'

Van Hopkins burst into laughter. 'That's a mystery itself. Maybe he has a ghost. Maybe his wife writes 'em. I wouldn't worry about it.'

They left the house. The morning was cool and clear, the sky sparkling blue. A soft breeze was blowing in off the Pacific. Claire settled herself in the Nash. She opened her purse and took a tiny slip of paper from it. Burt van Hopkins shot a glance at her and at the slip.

'You saved your fortune.'

She actually blushed and stammered an affirmative.

'Women are so sentimental,' van Hopkins commented.

'*Do not search for him, if it is fated you will find him,*' she quoted. She dropped the slip back into her purse and snapped it shut.

'I don't even remember mine,' van Hopkins said.

'I do. It was, '*A wise man seeks the advice of a wise woman.*''

'Silly tripe.'

'Not at all.'

Van Hopkins drove to the Mission

District. He and Claire checked a series of cafés and early-morning bars without success. When they tried the Tenderloin they had more luck. Van Hopkins dragged Claire Delacroix by the wrist into a darkened dive that smelled of bourbon and stale tobacco smoke. 'There he is,' van Hopkins whispered.

'Okay.' Claire wondered how van Hopkins had managed to recognize anybody in the murky saloon, but he led her to a rickety table where a man sat staring into space. He held a shot glass in one hand and a bottle in the other. It was hard to judge colors in the dim light but to Claire Delacroix it looked as if the man's face was grey. He wore a fedora on the back of his head, a black moustache on his upper lip, and a navy blue suit.

Van Hopkins pulled two bentwood chairs to the table. He held one for Claire Delacroix, like a perfect little gentleman, waited for her to sit down, then turned the other around and planted himself with his arms on the back of the chair.

'You're not holding a private wake for Happy Henry Previtali, are you, Bernie?'

Bernie Zapf looked at van Hopkins, then at Claire Delacroix. 'Who's the twist?'

'Now, Bernie, don't be impolite. This is Miss Delacroix. Say hello to Miss Delacroix.'

Van Hopkins had reached sideways and had his hand concealed in Zapf's ribs.

Zapf grunted and clutched his glass and his bottle more tightly. 'Hello, Miss Delacroix.' He spoke in a monotone. 'And no, I'm not grieving for Previtali, I wouldn't give two pins to save that — ' He ended the sentence with an expletive that surprised Claire Delacroix, not an easy thing to do.

'Okay,' van Hopkins said, 'the cops are out to find the clever soul who got rid of Henry. Somehow I think you'd be on their suspect list.'

'And why is that?'

'You're a peculiar fellow, Bernie. There are a lot of dubious characters in the book trade but you're the only collector I know with the connections you've got. You're the only one who could have arranged things the way they happened

314

up in North Beach.'

'Don't make me laugh. Why would I want to kill Henry? He was selling me what I wanted.'

Van Hopkins nodded. 'You've got a point. Why would a hop head kill his supplier?'

'I ain't no hop head, what's the matter with you, you don't know nothing, van Hopkins.'

'Oh, Bernie, you don't understand the art of metaphor, do you? How do you ever write your murder mysteries? Never mind, drink up and then I'll have another question or two for you.'

Zapf took van Hopkins' advice as far as drinking up. The bottle in his hand was a cheap brand of rye but at least it was probably not poisonous, now that Prohibition was gone. As for the rest of the matter, 'I wouldn't know a metaphor from a meatball, wise guy. I just tell stories. And why the hell should I answer your questions, van Hopkins? You're a lousy typewriter jockey, and I don't mean no Tommy gun.'

'Okay.' Van Hopkins slid backwards

and stood up. 'Come on, Claire. Cleland Baxter and the boys in the basement will talk to Bernie if Bernie won't talk to us.'

That got Zapf's attention. He jerked his eyes upward. 'What do you want, you louse?'

★　★　★

Akhenaton Beelzebub Chase sat up in bed and stretched. Sunlight was pouring through the windows of his suite atop the Palace Hotel. He had left the draperies open when he retired. A natural awakening as the sun's rays penetrated the early morning fog was far preferable to a shrill wake-up call from the hotel's front desk. The sound of automobile horns and streetcar bells rose faintly from busy Market Street.

He ordered his breakfast, showered and shaved and dressed. While he waited for his meal to arrive he reviewed the events of the previous evening.

Stuart Thielemann had been hugely relieved to see a uniformed police captain when he opened his door and not a gunman. He'd demanded to see Baxter's credentials but once convinced of the captain's legitimacy he willingly accompanied Baxter and Abel Chase to police headquarters and answered the questions put to him by a couple of Baxter's subordinates. He admitted that he had supplied the musical rarities to Previtali but he adamantly refused to reveal where he got them.

'Look, fellas,' he pleaded, 'I'd tell you in a minute, but bow long would I last? Somebody took care of Enrico, I was right there. Cripes, if the waiter had switched desserts I'd be on a slab right now and you'd be talking to him instead of me.'

Cleland Baxter spoke softly to Abel Chase. 'You need a drink, Dr. Chase. And I could use one myself. Come on, we'll relax upstairs for a bit while the boys here chat with Mr. Thieleman.'

Thielemann said, 'I heard that. Don't go upstairs, Captain. You stay here. You're a decent guy, everybody knows that, don't go upstairs, you know what these toughs will do as soon as you're out of the room.

317

Don't go upstairs, Cap.'

Baxter smiled. Thielemann was sitting on a hard chair. The only other furniture in the room was a scratched wooden table and a couple more chairs. Why should the inquisitors be less comfortable than their guest?

Baxter put his hand on Thielemann's shoulder. 'Don't be afraid, son. Didn't they teach you that in elementary school, *the policeman is my friend*. I'll be right upstairs with Dr. Chase. You just tell these nice fellows what they want to know and you'll be all right. We'll even provide a nice safe place for you to sleep tonight.'

Thielemann began to cry.

Baxter reached into his uniform pocket and pulled out a handkerchief. He handed it to the book scout. He took Abel Chase by the elbow and steered him toward the door.

An hour later the phone on Captain Baxter's desk rang. He held the earpiece close to his head, a puzzled expression on his face.

'You're sure?' he finally said. After a few more seconds he said, 'all right. Bring

318

him whatever he wants — a glass of water, coffee, some booze. But hold it back from him. He's all right, isn't he? Good. Yes, Dr. Chase and I will be right down.'

He hung the earpiece back on its hook and shot a quizzical look at Chase.

'What is it, Clel?'

Baxter shook his bead. 'Come on downstairs. I want you to hear this for yourself, not from me.'

Stuart Thielemann looked the worse for wear, but Baxter and Chase had seen far worse in the trenches of France and in hospital in England. Thielemann still had both his eyes and most of his teeth although his lips were swollen and split and it looked as if he had a shiner or two on the way.

He grinned up at Cleland Baxter. 'Real sweet boys you got working for you, Cap.'

There was a bottle of whiskey on the table, a jelly-jar glass, and, surprisingly, a bucket of ice cubes,

'Come on, Thielemann, let's make this all friendly.'

Baxter dropped a couple of ice cubes

into the glass. 'On the rocks for you, Mr. Thielemann? Yes? Good.' He poured some whiskey over the ice cubes, filled the glass and handed it to the scout.

Thielemann accepted the glass gratefully and took a generous swallow. He winced when the alcohol hit his lips but he smiled and wiped his mouth with the handkerchief that Baxter had handed him earlier. 'You want this back, Cap?'

Baxter smiled.

'With my compliments, Thielemann. A souvenir of your visit to San Francisco Police Headquarters. Is this your first? I hope you'll come see us many times.'

Thielemann grunted and emptied his glass. Only the ice cubes remained.

'Now,' Baxter said, 'I'd like you to tell me what you told my boys.'

Thielemann held the glass toward Baxter.

The captain took it, refilled it with whiskey, then set the glass down on the table. 'Okay, where did you get the manuscripts you sold to Enrico Previtali?'

'I got 'em on Nob Hill. Let me have another drink, Captain.'

'Sure thing, Thielemann. Where did you get the manuscripts?'

'Cap, I need a drink.'

'Poor fellow. Dr. Chase, would you care for some refreshment?'

He held the glass toward Abel Chase.

'No? I thought not. Beneath your taste. And I don't blame you, sir. Here, you fellows, get rid of this swill, will you?'

Thielemann tried to rise from his chair but two officers held him. 'You're a bastard, Baxter.'

The captain's eyes widened. 'Oh, oh, now you're getting nasty. All right, Dr. Chase, we have better stuff upstairs, let's go.'

'No! I'll tell you.'

Baxter waited.

'I already told these guys.'

'Tell me.'

'Loretta Hodge.'

Baxter was disappointed, or at least he managed to simulate disappointment. 'You must have misunderstood. We know that Mrs. Hodge was buying manuscripts from Previtali. And we know that Previtali was getting them from you. I'm sure you did nicely on them, and that Happy Henry did as well. And the good lord knows that Mrs. Hodge could afford *to* buy them. All very nice, everybody gets his piece of the pie and Mrs. Hodge winds up with her precious manuscript.'

During the pause that followed, there was no sound in the room except for the breathing of Abel Chase, Cleland Baxter, Stuart Thielemann, and two muscular police officers.

Finally, Thielemann said, 'No, Cap, honestly. You don't understand. I got the manuscripts from Mrs. Hodge.'

Baxter shook his head, shaggy iron-gray hair falling over his forehead. The top man in the homicide squad didn't have to abide by regulations about military-style haircuts.

'You're telling me that Mrs. Hodge sold you the manuscripts, you sold them to Enrico Previtali, and be sold them back to Mrs. Hodge.'

'That's right. Some of them. Bernie Zapf got some, too.'

'Bernie Zapf.'

'That's right.'

'Two bit mob man, claims he writes murder mysteries.'

'That's the guy.'

Baxter turned toward Abel Chase. 'What do you think, sir?'

Chase shrugged his shoulders. Even at the end of the long day and night, his clothing fit to perfection and looked far fresher than it must have felt.

'The what of crime is not nearly as strange and fascinating as the why.'

'Jeez,' Baxter muttered, 'I'm looking for facts and I get philosophy.'

To Stuart Thielemann he said, 'All right, my lad. I promised you a safe place to spend the night and I'll keep my word. Accommodations here aren't exactly the Sir Francis but you'll be safe and not too uncomfortable.' To the officers he said, 'Take him upstairs, boys. Give him a nice cozy cell.'

Thielemann stood up. This time no one stopped him. He started to protest but Baxter cut him off. 'If you want to decline our hospitality, that's your right, dear boy. You're not under arrest. Shall we turn you loose?'

For a moment the scout stood considering his choices. 'I wouldn't last an hour.'

'Maybe you would, maybe you wouldn't. The choice is yours, my lad,'

Thielemann frowned. 'All right.' He turned to the nearest officer. 'Show me a cell, pal. I'd like one with a northern exposure.' To Cleland Baxter he said, 'But would you do me just one big favor, Captain Baxter?'

Cleland Baxter nodded encouragingly.

'Please, Cap, just stop calling me *my lad*.'

The ferries had stopped running so Baxter offered Abel Chase a ride via police cruiser to the hotel of his choice, and he'd chosen the splendid semi-antique Palace.

* * *

The next morning Chase dined on grapefruit, toast, eggs, bacon, and coffee. The toast was locally baked sourdough, and it went well with marmalade.

The hotel valet had cleaned and

324

pressed Chase's outfit and had it ready by the time he had showered. His low cordovan shoes were meticulously cleaned and shined to a brilliance that would have pleased any drill instructor in the army. He had the desk send up a selection of morning newspapers and was scanning them for reports of the Previtali case when his telephone rang.

It was Cleland Baxter.

'Giordano is dead.'

'Who?'

'Alcide Giordano. I thought you never forgot anything, Dr. Chase. Alcide Giordano was the waiter who served Enrico Previtali the fatal cannoli at Tommasino's restaurant. Jeez, this thing is starting to sound like an Italian opera, ain't it?'

Chase lowered his coffee cup. 'What happened?'

'The guy must have figured that his employers would have somebody watching at the train station and the Ferry Building so he stole a car and beat it out of town. Not such a bad idea but he picked the wrong car. One of them new DeSoto Airflow buggies. Stuck out like a sore thumb. On top of that, the owner spotted him driving away and called the traffic squad. They put the license plate on the wire and the Highway Patrol spotted him down on the Peninsula. They chased him as far as Half Moon Bay and the poor galoot went over a cliff. Smashed the DeSoto to smithereens and splattered the guy all over the rocks.'

Abel Chase pondered that. 'Too bad. The waiter was just a pawn in this game but be could have connected us to the real players. All right, we still have the scout Thielemann in hand and we have our leads to Previtali's customers, Zapf and Mrs. Hodge.'

'I have some boys out looking for Zapf right now,' Baxter told him. 'As for the widow Hodge, I don't want to bring her in. She's too rich, she'll probably refuse to cooperate and if I have to detain her as a material witness there'll be hell to pay from City Hall and the Chief's office. No, I'm going out to St. Francis Woods with my hat in my hand and see what I can get out of her.'

Chase agreed with Baxter's strategy. He

volunteered to accompany Baxter and his offer was taken up. Shortly thereafter he was seated with Baxter in the backseat of a powerful police cruiser. Officer Mulrooney was behind the wheel once again. Cleland Baxter had already given Mulrooney his directions. Loretta Hamilton Hedge's mansion in St. Francis Wood was one of the original Gutterson structures, built a quarter century before in the Italian Renaissance style. The wide lawn was perfectly tended and a pair of tall Washington palms flanked a gravel driveway. A nude nymph rose from a marble fountain in the center of the lawn. Anyone standing beneath the front portico of the house could look out on Lake Merced and beyond it the Pacific Ocean.

Baxter parked the police cruiser behind a huge Marmon Sixteen.

Moments later Captain Cleland Baxter and Dr. Akhenaton Beelzebub Chase stood at the front door.

Baxter raised a heavy iron knocker and pounded once on its iron striker plate. Abel Chase was surprised when the door swung open. He and Baxter had waited longer than either of them might have expected, and now they were greeted not by the expected servant but by Mrs. Hodge herself.

At least, Abel Chase was fairly sure the person was Loretta Hamilton Hodge. He did not mix much with San Francisco society, preferring the academic world and the intellectual companionship of his colleagues at the University of California. But he did look at the Sunday rotogravure sections on occasion, and the marcelled blonde hair, pale eyes and powdered visage of the woman matched his recollection of the images in the newspapers.

She opened the door and staggered backwards for a step. Cleland Baxter reached forward and clutched her hands. 'Are you all right, Madam?'

She shook her head and babbled something indistinguishable. Baxter and Abel Chase entered the vestibule with her, then halted. The vestibule let onto a magnificent front room, its terrazzo floor partially covered with Persian carpets.

Stained glass windows cast colored beams over furniture that could only have come from a Venetian *palazzo* of some prior century.

But neither the police captain nor the academic had time to admire the furnishings of the house. Instead they faced a pair of serge-suited toughs pointing revolvers. One of the toughs growled at his partner, 'Get the cop's heater.' To Baxter and Chase he barked, 'Hands up and no tricks. You know the drill. Jeez, that's Captain Baxter, ain't it? Yes, I'd know that mug anywhere. You know me, Baxter?'

The captain said, 'I recognize you. I recognize both of you. Listen, fellows, you'd better lay down your guns right now and let me take you in. You don't have a chance, you know. We'll get to the bottom of this and maybe you can talk things over with the district attorney.'

The second gunman had patted Baxter down, removing his Webley Bulldog and shoving it into his coat pocket. 'What about this other gink?' the crook asked his partner.

'Check him out.'

'I carry no weapons save my mind,' Abel Chase said.

'Yeah, right. Don't move.' He ran his hands over Chase's jacket and trousers. 'Nothin',' he told his partner.

'Of course not,' Chase muttered.

'All right.' The senior crook took over. He wore a black fedora, a dark shirt under his serge suit and a yellow tie.

'Look, you two, you walked in at a very bad time. Now just sit down over there.' He pointed to an Italianate sofa. 'We'll figure out what to do with you.'

To his partner he growled. 'Tie 'em up.'

Where the mobster got the rope that he used, Abel Chase could not fathom, unless the likes of these two carried hemp with them for all occasions.

Within minutes he was sitting beside Cleland Baxter, his hands bound behind him and his ankles tied together. Baxter's condition was no different from Chase's.

'All right, darling,' the senior crook said to Mrs. Hodge, 'Make it easy on yourself. You just direct us to your treasures. We'll leave you these two pals for playmates and be on our way.'

'I don't believe you. I don't trust you. I hired you to work for me and you've turned on me. I don't believe you'll keep your word. Once I show you everything, I — I don't know what you'll do and I don't want to find out.'

'But we've kept our word,' the mobster said.

Was he trying sweet reason, Abel Chase wondered? And was Mrs. Hodge alone in her home? Wouldn't there be at least a modest staff of servants, perhaps a butler, a chauffeur, a cook, a maid and a laundress? Where were they?

That was of no concern. They weren't at hand, and these gunmen were in charge. 'I wouldn't trust them, Mrs. Hodge. The only thing keeping you alive is the fact that you have something they want. If you let them have it they won't need you any longer. They won't need any of us.'

The junior gunman ordered, 'Shut up!' He swung his weapon at Abel Chase, the heavy cylinder of the revolver smashing into Chase's skull high above the ear.

Chase still wore his fedora; its heavy felt cushioned the blow but did not stop it from causing blackness to drop in front of Chase's eyes. It lasted only a moment; he felt himself collide, shoulder-to-shoulder, with Cleland Baxter, then tumble onto the carpet. He lay there staring at the high ceiling. It was decorated with a painting of cherubs and virgins.

A sharp-toed shoe dug into Chase's ribs. 'Don't try and get up.'

He could only moan in reply.

A voice sounded from the vestibule. Chase's ears were ringing from the blow he had received, and he could see only part of what was going on. Mrs. Hodge made a dash for the front of the house. One of the gunmen brought her down with a flying tackle worthy of Bronko Nagurski. The other raised his revolver and fired once, ran past Chase and Baxter and disappeared from Chase's field of vision. Two more shots echoed from the marble walls and terrazzo floor.

'Jeez,' Chase heard the junior gangster's voice, 'You killed him. You killed a cop. We're really in the soup now.'

'His tough luck. What was he, Baxter, you left him outside?'

Baxter gritted, 'He was just a glorified chauffeur, you morons. You'll swing for this, there's no way out for you now.'

'Really?' The senior gunman stood over Baxter. Abel Chase could hear Mrs. Hodge snuffling. He couldn't see her, had no way of knowing whether she was seriously injured or merely suffering from terror and from shock. 'If we're gonna hang anyhow, I don't suppose it matters if we kill you and your pansy friend, Baxter. By the way, I always thought you liked girls. Well, live and learn.'

'Why?' Baxter asked.

A puzzled expression appeared on the gunman's face. Abel Chase could see him now. His vision had cleared but his ears still rang and his head felt as if he'd taken a pounding from the great Henry Armstrong.

'Why did you get into this mess?'

Chase turned his head. The gangster was standing over Cleland Baxter, a bemused expression on his vicious face. 'What do you care? You're not going to be around much longer, Baxter.'

The captain shook his head. 'Maybe I'm just curious.'

'You mean why did we have Alcide Giordano get rid of the book-dealer? Mrs. Hodge here paid us. Hey, we're just honest working men, we offer our service to the public and good citizens who don't want to get their hands dirty give us jobs. It pays better than pumping gas and wiping windshields, don't it, Mrs. Hodge? You know what? It even pays better than running cooze and hop.'

Chase heard the woman groan.

'But why? Mrs. Hodge was a customer of Previtali's. Why would she want him dead?'

'Hey, ask her yourself.'

Chase saw the gangster motion to his partner. Shortly the second man reappeared, pushing the no-longer-elegant Loretta Hamilton Hodge before him. He shoved her into a chair. She sat with her face in her hands.

'Why, Mrs. Hodge?'

She raised her face. Tears were running down her cheeks, tracing rivulets in the thick powder. 'For the Mozart,' she said.

'For the Mozart? What?'

How could Cleland Baxter and Loretta Hamilton Hodge carry on this conversation when they were both about to be shot? It was all very strange, but Abel Chase had seen actions as strange in the trenches of France, frightened men racing through letters from their sweethearts before pulling on gasmasks as noxious fumes poured over them, dying men settling quarrels over Woodrow Wilson versus Charles Evans Hughes in the election of 1916, the Boston Red Sox versus the Chicago Cubs in the World Series of 1918.

'He wouldn't sell the Mozart holograph for any price. I offered the man a fortune and he wouldn't budge. I thought I could get it from him by giving him my treasures. The Talus, the Brahms. There were others. I knew there would be no use in trying to arrange a trade. So I let that awful scout Stuart Thielemann have some good items to prime Previtali with money. You know, Captain Baxter, there's nothing like wealth to make

335

people want more wealth.'

'I wouldn't know,' Baxter said.

'It's true, Captain, take my word for it. I thought once he saw how much money he could make by furnishing connoisseurs with true wonders instead of the trinkets he's always peddled, he would decide to make his big killing by selling me the Mozart. He still refused. So I had him killed. Surely there will be an estate sale and then I'll get the aria.'

There was a moment of silence, a silence that might be broken at any moment by the sound of gunfire. But instead, Cleland Baxter asked, 'Where did you get the manuscripts you sold to Thielemann?'

'Oh, Captain.' Mrs. Hodge smiled happily, her wrinkled face looking for a moment like a child learning that she is to receive just the Christmas gift she most desired. 'It's easy if you have enough money. All you have to do is put the word out that you're looking for something and you're willing to pay any price, and it comes to you. Would you like a Titian, a Breughel, a Vermeer? A Michelangelo

sculpture? A Fabergé Egg? A golden
scarab from the tomb of Tutankhamun?
Anything is possible, Captain. All you
need is a checkbook. Almost anything is
possible. Even a Mozart holograph.'

★ ★ ★

Burt van Hopkins pulled the Nash coupé
to a halt behind the San Francisco police
cruiser and the huge Marmon sedan. He
shook his head. 'I don't like this. Something nasty is going on inside the house.'

He put his hand on Claire Delacroix's
wrist. 'Wait here, I'm going to find out
what's happening.

'I'm coming, too.'

'No, Claire. Please. I know what I'm
doing.'

She didn't want to quarrel. Against her
better judgment she decided to let him go
— first, not alone. But, 'Here, take this.'

But he was already out of the coupé,
sprinting up the polished stone path. She
saw him hurry up the marble steps. The
great door of the mansion stood open.
What that meant, Claire Delacroix could

not fathom, save to realize that it boded ill.

Burt van Hopkins set foot in the vestibule of the Hodge mansion. For a moment his eyes were unable to adjust to the darkened chamber. Then he saw the scene before him and started forward. Something hard and heavy crashed against the side of his head and he plummeted to the floor.

Two shots rang out in rapid succession and the gunmen standing in the luxurious chamber fell. The junior of the two, his back to the entryway, toppled without a sound. The senior gunman was facing the entryway. He had time to raise his own revolver but the heavy round from Enrico Previtali's five-shot Adams revolver struck him in the center of the chest with so much force he literally left his feet. An involuntary grunt escaped him, then he crashed against the marble fireplace, twitched once, and lay still.

Claire Delacroix ran to Burt van Hopkins. The journalist was moaning and trying to raise himself. His tweed cap was soaked with blood. From some long-ago lesson, Claire Delacroix remembered that the scalp was rich in blood vessels, that a bloody wound did not necessarily mean a serious injury. She looked into van Hopkins' eyes and saw the brightness of consciousness and recognition. She grabbed a silk arabesque pillow and slid it under his head.

She found the kitchen and while she was at it she found the missing Hodge servants. She averted her eyes from the sight. She returned to the main room with a carving knife and used it to free Abel Chase and Cleland Baxter.

Baxter rubbed his wrists to restore circulation. He took Mrs. Hodge by both hands. He said, 'You are under arrest for murder and for conspiracy to commit murder.' He hesitated, watching her eyes. Then he added, 'I'm very sorry, Mrs. Hodge. The District Attorney will settle all the details.'

★ ★ ★

Akhenaton Beelzebub Chase and Claire Delacroix sat at the great hand-carved table in Chase's mansion. The sun was setting behind the Golden Gate, suffusing the room with a warm glow and the illusion of a smoky perfume. Both had bathed and changed to lounging costumes.

Chase's head was partially wrapped in linen windings and sticking plasters.

Leicester Jenkins had prepared a simple meal for them. A bowl of lamb stew stood before each of them, a glass of Chardonnay beside each.

'A sad case, Delacroix, sad.' Abel Chase swallowed some Chardonnay, then smiled broadly. 'I had not realized you were so handy with firearms. You brought down those two thugs with two shots. What shall we call you now, Dead-Eye Delacroix?'

'I would prefer not.'

A low-lying fog had swept in from the ocean and San Francisco Bay, and was slowly creeping up the hillside below the mansion.

'There are a good many things you don't know about me, Dr. Chase.'

'The revolver you used — it was Enrico

Previtali's, was it not?'

'It was.'

'I suppose, then it was technically stolen property.'

'Oh, I'm really not worried about being charged with theft, Dr. Chase. What matters more is that you were not seriously hurt,' Claire Delacroix lifted her glass in one elegant hand and took a small sip of wine. 'Nor was Burt van Hopkins. Captain Baxter is unharmed and Officer Mulrooney will recover.'

'True. But the Hodge servants — there was no need to slaughter them. Those gangsters could have tied them, locked them in the pantry. What did they hope to gain by holding Mrs. Hodge as a hostage, anyway?'

'I'm sure they thought she would turn over her own collection of holographs. It wouldn't be easy to sell such stolen goods, but they would have found buyers somehow, and the manuscripts are worth a fortune.'

Chase nodded.

'But Alcide Giordano is dead, Enrico Previtali is dead, the two mobsters are dead, Mrs. Hodge's employees are dead. Have I left anyone out?'

Chase said, 'I think not.'

'And what will become of Mrs. Hodge?'

Claire Delacroix held her glass at eye level and gazed through it at the setting sun. Gold viewed through gold.

Abel Chase echoed her question. 'What will become of Mrs. Hodge?'

THE END

We do hope that you have enjoyed reading this large print book.

Did you know that all of our titles are available for purchase?

We publish a wide range of high quality large print books including:
Romances, Mysteries, Classics
General Fiction
Non Fiction and Westerns

Special interest titles available in large print are:
The Little Oxford Dictionary
Music Book, Song Book
Hymn Book, Service Book

Also available from us courtesy of Oxford University Press:
Young Readers' Dictionary
(large print edition)
Young Readers' Thesaurus
(large print edition)

For further information or a free brochure, please contact us at:
Ulverscroft Large Print Books Ltd.,
The Green, Bradgate Road, Anstey,
Leicester, LE7 7FU, England.
Tel: (00 44) **0116 236 4325**
Fax: (00 44) **0116 234 0205**

Other titles in the
Linford Mystery Library:

SNAKE EYES

Richard Hoyt

John Denson, the Seattle private eye with his partner, Willie Prettybird — a shaman of the Cowlitz tribe — face their deadliest case: an engineered outbreak of anthrax in the Pacific Northwest. A ballooning list of suspects includes a rodeo cowboy; a barkeep with a roving eye; an ancient teacher at a high-school reunion — and the chief of police. Then there's the fund-raising televangelist Hamm Bonnerton. One of them is playing liar's dice, and coming up snake eyes. And killing people . . .

TERROR LOVE

Norman Lazenby

Married to Gilbert Brand, Kathryn imagines her marriage to be a happy one. It's studded with the parties of her husband's rich, socialite friends. But their attendance at a party given by his business associate, Victor Milo, tarnishes Brand's suave image. Kathryn discovers Brand attempting to strangle another guest, the nightclub singer Claudia, who becomes Kathryn's bitterest enemy. Then her world begins to crumble as she learns that Brand is an unscrupulous criminal . . . and she begins a descent into terror.

THE MING VASE

E. C. Tubb

Inside Cartwright House, a secret Government military project takes place. Men and women are well cared for, with every leisure facility. But they are prisoners, forbidden to leave. Their defection to, or capture by, foreign powers could be catastrophic. These people have very special powers, capable of being harnessed by enemies who could threaten and destroy western civilization. So when Klieger does escape, Special C.I.A. agent Don Gregson must find him. The only clue? Klieger has stolen a Ming vase.